that is **sal**
1 can ke

i fixed he ... my
of a solution,' he said calmly.

ell, I don't like it.'

what do you suggest, then?' He looked at
with a raised eyebrow. 'Do you think it
uld be better if I wait until the child is born
take you forcibly to court because I want
tody?'

u wouldn't do that?' Her breath seemed to
ze in her throat.

itie, I'll do whatever it takes,' he told her
verfully. 'And, believe me, you don't want
)e on the wrong side of me. Because I have
money and resources to go all the way, and
ill win...'

Kathryn Ross was born in Zambia, where her parents happened to live at that time. Educated in Ireland and England, she now lives in a village near Blackpool, Lancashire. Kathryn is a professional beauty therapist, but writing is her first love. As a child she wrote adventure stories, and at thirteen was editor of her school magazine. Happily, ten writing years later, DESIGNED WITH LOVE was accepted by Mills & Boon®. A romantic Sagittarian, she loves travelling to exotic locations.

KEPT BY HER GREEK BOSS

BY
KATHRYN ROSS

MILLS & BOON
Pure reading pleasure™

All the characters in this book have no existence outside the imagination of the author, and have no relation whatsoever to anyone bearing the same name or names. They are not even distantly inspired by any individual known or unknown to the author, and all the incidents are pure invention.

First published in Great Britain 2009
Harlequin Mills & Boon Limited,
Eton House, 18-24 Paradise Road, Richmond, Surrey TW9 1SR

© Kathryn Ross 2009

ISBN: 978 0 263 87207 1

Set in Times Roman 10½ on 12¾ pt
01-0509-49011

Printed and bound in Spain
by Litografia Rosés, S.A., Barcelona

KEPT BY HER
GREEK BOSS

PROLOGUE

KATIE glanced out of the window and watched the sun setting in a pink, misty haze over the London rooftops. Maybe she wasn't pregnant, she told herself fiercely. She was only a week late, and she was never regular anyway.

She should go take the test right now. Her eyes skidded towards her bag, and her heart thundered with apprehension. Now that the phones had stopped ringing and the offices were deserted, it was the perfect time.

The sooner she knew, the sooner she could make a decision as to what she should do.

And what would she do if this test were positive?

She leaned her forehead against the cool of the glass.

There was no doubt that her boss was the most handsome, exciting man she had ever met, or that she had been enjoying their affair. But that was all it was—an *affair*.

Alexi wasn't the settling-down type; he'd made that absolutely clear from the beginning. And she'd been OK with that. In fact, more than OK; she'd agreed wholeheartedly.

She'd thought she had it all worked out—all under control, she mocked herself as she straightened and turned her back on the view.

Now suddenly she was looking at her affair with Alexi

in a whole different way, and what she was seeing, and what she was feeling, was scaring her.

It was strange how life could change in an instant.

She was about to pick up her bag when a noise in the outer office alerted her to the fact that she wasn't alone, and she looked up to find Alexi standing in the doorway.

As always her senses flew into wild disorder as their eyes met. 'Crushingly handsome' was how she had once described the Greek tycoon, and that description was extremely apt.

'You do realise that everyone else has finished for the day, don't you?' he asked.

'I had some figures to check,' she retorted, trying to focus her mind on business, sitting back in her chair.

'So, how's it going?'

'I'm nearly finished. Another few days and the deal will be signed and sealed.' Another few days and her contract here would be finished.

Her eyes drifted over him as he walked closer. She liked the way he dressed; he had the stylish panache that continental men seemed to achieve so effortlessly. But that wasn't what drew her—nor was it the tall, muscular, toned body beneath the clothes—it was something else. It was that aura of power that he wore so well, that cool, confident, almost ruthless way he had of holding her attention. She wished that he didn't have an effect on her, and that he didn't send her senses into free fall, but he did.

Hurriedly she tried to put those emotions away as he stopped in front of her desk.

'You've done well. Of course, it means we're going to have to set aside some time to talk about where things are going from here.'

Did he mean emotionally? She swallowed hard and couldn't find her voice to reply.

'I'd like you to stay on.'

His quietly spoken words opened up feelings inside her that she didn't dare try to analyse. Instead she looked up at him cautiously, and her whole body seemed to be tensing, waiting. 'In what capacity?'

'Same as now. I'm buying a new company, and I'd like you to oversee a similar project for me.'

She tried to ignore the curl of disappointment. Of course he hadn't been talking in emotional terms. Alexi never discussed emotions; they were a definite taboo. He was a businessman first and foremost.

'And what about...us?' She forced herself to ask the question.

'Well, we can carry on as before, can't we?' His dark eyes held with hers, and then he smiled. 'Enjoying ourselves.'

She nodded and tried to look casually indifferent. 'Well, we can discuss it later.'

He frowned for a moment as if he hadn't been expecting that. 'So the next question is...' he leaned forward and put his hands on her desk '...your place or mine?'

The smooth transition from businessman to lover made Katie's stomach-muscles tighten. She wanted him so much...wanted to push everything to one side and just go into his arms and be held.

But Alexi didn't intend to just hold her; he intended to make love to her until she was senseless and sated beyond belief. Then he'd smile that satisfied smile and tell her she was great, before moving away and turning the conversation and the mood back towards business.

For the first time in their relationship Katie felt like she couldn't handle that situation. The knowledge swirled inside her with disquieting intensity.

'I thought you had a meeting with the director of Transworth tonight?' She played for time.

'Yes, but it shouldn't last long. I'll be finished by about ten.' He came round to her side of the desk and perched beside her.

His closeness unsettled her even more. 'Alexi, it's been a crazy day today. I haven't stopped, and—'

'Are you bailing out on me?' He didn't sound annoyed, just amused.

'Afraid so.' She couldn't meet his gaze. 'A girl has to catch up on her beauty sleep some time.'

He reached out and tipped her chin upwards, so that she was forced to look at him, and she was glad that the light in the office was fading now. His gaze was too perceptive— almost as if he could read the secrets of her soul.

'You look pretty hot for a woman in need of her beauty sleep.' He murmured the words huskily, and the touch of his hand against her skin made her feel weak with longing. 'But I'll let you off tonight as long as you think about my business proposition.'

'You are such a smooth talker, Alexi.' She tried to sound flippant.

He didn't immediately release her. Instead his fingers stroked softly upwards, tracing along the delicate heart-shape of her face and into the darkness of her long hair.

She took a deep, shuddering breath as he lowered his head and took possession of her lips.

Hell, but he could kiss… He had a way of lighting her up inside, making her want him with an urgency she had never experienced before. Over the last couple of months she had allowed herself to surrender to him completely, had loved the wild, exhilarating feelings he created inside her— but today his mastery over her senses just scared her.

She didn't want to feel like this any more, she thought hazily, yet she couldn't stop herself leaning forward and giving herself up to the pleasure of the moment.

His mobile phone rang, shattering the silence. For a moment he ignored it, before abruptly pulling away. 'Sorry, Katie, I better take this call.'

She shrugged and tried not to care.

'Hi, Mark, what's the situation at the New York office?'

How was he able to kiss with such passion and then sound perfectly controlled the next moment?

Because he didn't connect with her on an emotional level—she answered her own question and tried to pull herself together.

This was no good—she needed to regain control. She smoothed her hair back from her face, and reached to pick up her handbag.

'Won't be long,' she murmured as she caught Alexi's eye.

He nodded. 'Just deal with it, Mark,' he snapped. 'I don't give second chances—the guy has messed up.'

Katie headed down the corridor. Alexi was a ruthless businessman; she knew that. But she'd also read enough about him in the gossip columns to know he could be ruthless in his private life, too.

He'd been married once, and since his divorce he'd changed his women with the weather.

If this pregnancy test was positive, she was going to be on her own. She was already aware of the rumour that his marriage had ended because he hadn't wanted children and his ex-wife had.

And *their* affair meant nothing to him!

How could she have been so stupid?

She'd grown up in a single-parent family, and it had been tough. Even now the memories haunted her.

If the test was negative she would learn her lesson, she promised herself fiercely. And she would finish with Alexi once and for all.

CHAPTER ONE

KATIE walked into the impressive foyer of the Madison Brown building with a feeling of excitement. It was the first day of her new job, and she couldn't wait to start.

It had taken her a month to find this position—a month of sifting through the many job offers and holding her nerve until the perfect post had come her way. Just in time, as well, because being within the solitude of her apartment had started to become like some kind of torture. Being alone every day had given her too much time to think about Alexi—to miss Alexi—and she didn't want to do that.

Even the thought of his name now made a feeling of pain rise inside her, and angrily she tried to stifle it. She was being ridiculous. She'd known the score, and she'd done exactly the right thing in leaving Demetri Shipping, and exactly the right thing in finishing with Alexi.

'Hi.' She smiled at the receptionist, who looked up at her. 'Katie Connor, new project manager.'

'Ah, yes, Ms Connor. Go on up to the top floor. The new managing director wants to talk to you before you start.'

Katie headed for the lifts and tried to ignore the sudden quiver of first-day nerves. Everything would be fine, she told herself firmly. They'd practically headhunted her for this job. The employment agency had told her that she was the only one on their books to have been selected for an interview. And the guy who'd rung to offer the job had told her the interview panel had been impressed with her level of experience. Obviously the fact that she had managed such a successful project at Demetri Shipping had paid off. He'd then told her that, by the time she started work, Madison Brown would be a satellite company of a big conglomerate called Tellesta.

She'd done her homework; she knew that Tellesta was a massive corporation, almost as big as Demetri Shipping.

There was going to be plenty of scope for her to develop her organisation skills—plus there was going to be the opportunity to travel to the sister offices in Paris and New York. She was looking forward to the excitement and the challenges that lay ahead.

The lift doors opened on the top floor, and she walked to the desk at the far end of the room where a young woman was switching on her computer and sorting through the morning post.

'Hi, my name is Katie Connor, I'm—'

'The new project-manager.' The woman finished her sentence for her and smiled. 'I'm Claire; I've been told to show you to your office.'

Katie looked around her with interest as she followed the woman down a long corridor. The modern offices showed spectacular views across London. The boardroom they passed was vast, with state-of-the-art conference equipment. 'This place is fantastic,' Katie murmured, lingering at the door.

'All newly instated,' Claire informed her proudly. 'The new parent company completely gutted the place, and money was no object. There's even a heliport upstairs, for the bigwigs to fly in and out from the airport to save time.'

'Very impressive.'

'Yes, it is, isn't it?' Claire opened a door at the end of the corridor. 'This is yours.'

Katie could hardly believe her luck! It was a large corner-office with views along Canary Wharf. With difficulty she dragged her eyes away from the view and concentrated on the desk and the stack of files sitting on top of it.

'I was told to gather research material for you,' Claire murmured as she watched Katie flicking through the top layers of papers. 'And you are to attend a meeting in the boardroom at ten.'

'OK.' Katie nodded. 'I thought the managing director wanted a word first?'

'He did, but he's had to go down to one of his other companies. He said he'd see you in the boardroom. Oh, and he's asked if you will look at the pre-Christmas budget figures and prepare a preliminary report on how you think they can be improved. He wants you to run your ideas past the board.'

'He wants me to prepare the report before ten?' Katie felt her nerves start to stretch a little.

'Afraid so.' Claire pulled a face. 'He's a man in a hurry.'

'I'll say!'

As Claire left, Katie took off her suit jacket and hung it up on the hook beside the filing cabinets.

This was what she'd wanted, she told herself as she started to sort through the piles of paper, a job that would challenge her and take her mind off the past.

The excitement of her previous job had been almost addictive—*or had that been the excitement of being with Alexi?*

Swiftly she cut the thought and told herself that she had

missed the cut and thrust of working for a dynamic company for the last few weeks, that was all. Alexi had been a mistake. She flicked through the papers angrily and tried to concentrate. But for a few moments no matter how hard she tried all she could think about was Alexi. Alexi kissing her…Alexi caressing her, possessing her…

She closed her eyes and took a deep breath. Then she reminded herself how scared she had felt when she'd thought she was pregnant. Thank heaven that test had come back negative, because Alexi was definitely not into commitment. His business was his one and only priority.

He'd looked at her almost coldly when she'd told him she wasn't going to stay on with the company.

'Is this an emotional decision or a business one?' he'd asked.

'Does it matter?'

'Yes. Because if your reasons are emotional it means you are not thinking straight.'

His logic had been so typical of him that she'd laughed. 'So the only good reason is a business reason?'

'Basically, yes.' He'd watched her impassively. 'We had an understanding, didn't we? We've been enjoying a bit of fun together, but we both agreed it wouldn't cloud work issues.'

'And it hasn't.' She'd tipped her chin up and met his gaze defiantly. 'I don't want the job you are offering because it's time for me to move on. Our agreement has reached the end of the road. I want a fresh challenge.' She'd managed to sound as collected and calm as he was. But inside she'd been hurting.

Inside she was still hurting—because there'd been a part of her that wanted him to show her some ounce of feeling, some spark of tenderness.

But he hadn't. He'd just told her that he'd leave the job offer open for a while and to get in contact if she changed her mind. Then he'd wished her well for the future and walked away.

He hadn't been around when she'd cleared her desk for the last time; he'd been in the States on business.

If he'd cared he wouldn't have been able to stay away. He wouldn't have been able to put business first.

She glared down at the papers on her desk. Why was she wasting time thinking about Alexi, when she was under pressure to produce a vital report for her new boss? Her relationship with Alexi was over and she needed to be realistic about it. Of course he hadn't cared about her; she had always known that. They'd shared 'a bit of fun', as he'd so coolly liked to refer to it. Not love—just sex.

Katie pulled the papers closer and forced herself to study them. She was a twenty-four-year-old woman with a degree in economics, not a love-struck fool. She'd made a mistake, she'd thought she could handle a relationship without letting her emotions intervene, but it hadn't worked for her. Now she needed to get over it. She took a deep breath and pushed all the past thoughts out of her mind, and felt a surge of a relief as she looked at the files in front of her. Yesterday had gone.

She circled some figures that suddenly struck her as unusual and traced their pattern. Then she started to make notes.

At nine forty-five she had put together a rough preliminary report. It wasn't perfect, but it was the best she would be able to achieve given the time restraints. And she had a few interesting points she would be able to raise at the meeting.

With a few minutes to spare, she left her desk and went

down the hallway to get a drink from a water machine she'd noticed earlier.

There was a mirror next to the dispenser, and she glanced briefly in it to check her appearance. She had applied more make-up than usual to disguise the fact that she hadn't been sleeping well. Her blue eyes looked good with the extra smudge of taupe highlighter, and the brighter lipstick complemented her skin tones and contrasted well with the darkness of her hair, but it wasn't really her. She tended to favour a more natural look.

They are not employing you for your style, she told herself sharply as she turned back towards her office; *they are interested in your brain.*

Hopefully now she had started her new job she would get a better night's sleep. She swung through her office door and came to an abrupt halt. For a moment she thought she was in the wrong place because there was someone sitting behind her desk. She couldn't see who it was, because he'd swivelled the chair around towards the window. All she could see was his long legs stretching out to one side and his hand holding her phone. He had a bit of a nerve to make himself at home like that, she thought with a frown. And he'd been reading her notes, she realised suddenly, as she saw he was holding them in the other hand.

'Excuse me?' She cleared her throat. 'Can I help you?'

'I'll have to get back to you, Ryan. I have a new employee to deal with before our meeting convenes.' The brisk, businesslike voice was velvety warm with just a hint of a Mediterranean accent, and Katie recognised it at once.

With the recognition came a plummeting feeling of shock as the office chair swivelled around and she found herself face to face with the man who had turned her world upside down and inside out—Alexander Demetri. Her mouth went dry; her stomach seemed to tie itself into knots.

For a moment she wondered if she was imagining things. She held her breath and wondered if she had thought about him so much over the last few weeks that she had actually conjured him up in some kind of wild illusion.

Then he put the phone down, leaned back in the leather chair and looked at her.

'Hello, Katie.'

There was no mistaking that cool, sardonic tone, or the glint in the darkness of his eyes. This wasn't some kind of dream—it was a complete nightmare!

CHAPTER TWO

'WHAT on earth are you doing here?' Her voice was numb with disbelief and it made his lips curve in a wryly amused smile.

'Well, at the moment it looks like I'm employing you to do a job that you originally told me you didn't want. Strange old world, isn't it?'

He sounded so cool and calm, and by contrast Katie was anything but calm. There were a million emotions buzzing around inside her and she couldn't get a handle on any of them.

'I don't understand,' she murmured. 'The job you offered me was with Demetri Shipping, wasn't it?'

'Demetri Shipping now owns Tellesta and Madison Brown,' he informed her. 'I bought them both out and took control about six weeks ago.' As he spoke Alexi allowed his eyes to rake over her. She looked good, he thought distractedly. Everything about her appearance was businesslike, from the white, crisp blouse to the black pencil-skirt. Yet there was an overt sexiness about her—the wide belt that emphasised her small waist, the hint of red gloss on her lips. She always had been too damn sexy for his peace of mind.

Aware of his scrutiny, Katie could feel herself tensing up even more. She wondered what he was thinking…was there even a small part of him that was glad to see her? Even as she asked the question she was berating herself for being a damn fool. Alexi didn't reason like that. She was just a notch on his bedpost, for heaven's sake!

'So, you had just finalised the deal to buy this place when…?' She almost said 'when we were together', but stopped before making that mistake. 'When I was working for you?' she finished instead. They had never been together, she reminded herself, not in the true sense of the word. Not as a couple.

He nodded.

'I didn't realize. I mean, when I applied for the job here, I didn't know it was with you.'

'I've gathered that.'

He was so damn cavalier! she thought angrily. Just *once* she'd like to see that arrogant, businesslike persona slip.

But the thing that made her really angry was that there *was* a part of her that was glad to see him. She hated that! It was the weak side of her nature, she told herself sternly, because she was over Alexander Demetri, well and truly over him.

OK—she still found him attractive—but then she would have to be dead not to find those dynamic, forceful good looks a turn on. Every woman with a pulse was attracted to him.

She tried not to look at him too closely, tried not to notice little things like the fact that his thick, dark hair had grown slightly and now just brushed the top of the midnight-blue jacket collar, the fact that there was a slight shadow on the strong jawline, or the sensual, almost cruel curve of his lips. Because when she noticed things like that she remembered how it had felt when he'd kissed her, when he'd crushed her against him, his skin abrasive against the softness of hers, his lips hungry and powerfully compelling.

'Did you know it was going to be me today?' she asked him suddenly. 'Did you know I had this job?'

'Of course!' He seemed to find the question amusing. 'Your name was put on my desk nearly a week ago.'

'So what are we going to do about this, Alexi?' For a second there was a raw, unguarded note in her voice. 'I can't work for you again.'

His eyes narrowed on her and a strange emotion sizzled through him, an emotion he couldn't place.

He supposed it was anger. Even though he knew he had no right to the emotion, he'd been furious when she'd turned down his offer to stay within the company and then casually walked away. That fury hadn't diminished any over the last few weeks. In fact if anything it had increased. Alexi was used to getting what he wanted—used to people dancing to his tune. And Katie had left before he was ready to let her go.

'I'm surprised that you feel like that.' He paused and measured his words. 'I expected you to be more...professional about this. You have just signed a four-month contract to work for Madison Brown. You must want the job.'

She glared at him. How dared he accuse her of being unprofessional? She wanted to tell him that he hadn't exactly been acting in accordance with the rules of business when he'd taken her to bed! But she held the words back; there was no point in raking over the past, and besides he'd probably point out that she had been as much to blame for what had happened as he was. And he'd be right. 'Yes, I wanted the job!' she said instead, her voice tightly controlled. 'But that was before I realised you owned the company!'

'What difference does that make?' He shrugged. 'I haven't got a problem with employing you again—so where's your difficulty?'

She could feel panic rising inside her like a gushing, icy spring. He didn't have a problem with it because his emotions weren't involved and hers were—not in a deep way, she reassured herself swiftly. But nevertheless she couldn't turn herself off to what had happened between them, couldn't deal with it in the same practical way that he obviously could. This was one of the reasons she had turned down his job offer last time.

He could probably deal with this because he was used to it, she realised numbly, used to taking a woman to bed and then dismissing her from his mind—whereas she was totally inexperienced at this kind of thing. In fact that whole casual-sex thing had been completely out of character for her. She'd only ever had one previous lover.

But she couldn't tell him that.

'I haven't got a problem with it—I just wanted to move on,' she told him.

Alexi watched as she lifted her chin in that determined way of hers, and something inside him twisted. He was usually the one to tell a woman when it was time to move on. This was the second time that Katie had dealt with him in this offhand manner, and he didn't like it. He didn't like it at all. 'You know, Katie, you and I used to have a good arrangement. It suited us both.'

'Yes, well, people change, don't they, Alexi? What suits one moment doesn't the next.'

'Very true.' His eyes narrowed on her. 'And it just makes me realise how very alike you and I are.'

Katie wanted to disagree vehemently, but she held her tongue.

'And we are both in agreement that we've enjoyed our fun and now we're moving on.' He shrugged again. 'I don't have a problem with that, Katie. I wanted you for this job because I believe you are the best person for it. It's just business.'

'I realise that!' She glared at him. 'I just wasn't sure that *you* did!'

For a second she was gratified to see a flare of something in his eyes—fury, or maybe just irritation; she wasn't sure. But she had struck some kind of response that had ruffled his impassive façade, and she was glad, so glad that it gave her a buzz of elation.

However, the feeling was short-lived, because then he just shrugged once more. 'I can reassure you that my first priority is work, Katie. It always has been and it always will be.'

The words upset her. They shouldn't have done—she knew he was just speaking the truth; she knew the score— but all the same it did hurt, and it crushed her brief feeling of triumph over him.

'Well, I suppose that's all right, then.' What else could she say? she asked herself as she tried to regain her composure and not lose her pride.

'Good.' His lips twisted in a sudden smile. 'So, now we have cleared the air, we can begin again.'

Begin again…? Katie wasn't sure she liked the sound of that. It made her nerves stretch, and she didn't know what to say. The reality of her situation was hitting her like a truck travelling at speed.

She had signed a contract for four months—she was effectively trapped here like a butterfly in a jar. *And the wonderful new job that was supposed to help her move on and forget the past had just turned to dust.*

'So, shall we get down to business now?' He glanced at his watch. 'There is a board meeting in about five minutes. Do you want to run through this report with me?' He tapped the piece of paper she had made notes on.

Fury raged through her. She hated him in that instant—hated his cool attitude, his arrogance, his disregard for even the smallest feeling of sentiment.

'I'm happy to run through it at the meeting,' she said tightly.

'Such confidence.'

'Your company is employing me because I'm good at what I do. I don't need any special favours.'

'I wasn't offering any. But the project you will be working on is of significant value. I thought it would be helpful for both of us to discuss a few points before the meeting.'

In other words he probably wouldn't even have walked in to see her today, only for the fact that her work was of interest to him.

'There isn't time for an in-depth debate now, Alexi; if there are any comments you want to make you can make them during the meeting.'

'OK.' Alexi's lips curved. He admired her brain, liked the way she could operate under pressure. He'd deliberately tested her this morning, asking for this report at short notice. And as always she had risen to the challenge. From the notes he had read he could see she had already picked up the gauntlet and was running with it. And that would please the board. 'A word of warning; you might meet with some resistance this morning. Some of the members of the board have concerns about the fact that you are rather young for such a major assignment.'

'I see.' Katie tried very hard not to show any concern. 'That's rather bizarre, isn't it? In today's world people in their early twenties are very successful, and I have plenty of experience.'

'Certainly.' He inclined his head. 'Don't worry about it. I have the last say, anyway.'

'I'm not worried about it. I'll deal with it.'

Alexi inclined his head. 'I'm sure you will.'

'Well, I think we've said all that needs to be said.' Katie glanced at her watch. She needed to get rid of him and gather her thoughts. 'I'll follow you down to the board-room in a few moments. I just want to highlight some points so I can read my notes more easily.'

Alexi shrugged and got up from behind the desk.

She'd almost forgotten how tall he was. Katie wasn't of diminutive stature herself, but he had to be about six foot three; he towered over her and seemed to dominate the room as he came closer. Every nerve ending in her body went on red alert as he stopped next to her. 'By the way, nice to have you back.' He murmured the words almost sardonically.

She wanted to tell him that she wasn't at all glad to be 'back', as he put it, and that she was working for him again under complete sufferance, but she forced herself just to nod.

He smiled as if he knew exactly what she'd been thinking. 'I'll see you in the boardroom.'

As soon as the door closed behind him, Katie felt like curling up and dying. She felt physically sick. How had she managed to make such an almighty *faux pas*? She'd re-searched Madison Brown—why hadn't any of the financial papers reported the fact that it had been taken over by Demetri Shipping? How had this happened to her?

She sat down at her desk and took deep breaths, trying to calm herself. There was no point panicking; it wasn't going to solve anything. She was just going to have to deal with the situation as best she could; after all, it was only for four months.

Another wave of panic hit her—*four months!* How was she going to keep up this cool, businesslike façade around him for that long when he sent every emotion in her body spinning into total chaos?

How long would it be before he smiled at her, touched her again, and sent common sense flying?

That wasn't going to happen, she told herself heatedly— she wasn't going to make the same mistake twice. She stared down at the papers in front of her. In two minutes she needed to be under perfect control and ready to face a boardroom of hostile people. This job should be her priority—not Alexi.

And anyway she probably wouldn't see that much of him. He was running three companies now, not one. Plus he probably already had a new girlfriend. It didn't take him long to replace a woman—they'd be queuing up.

She remembered suddenly how her mother had always fallen for the wrong men—the heartbreakers, the users— never the gentle, caring, commitment types. She remembered how she had always sworn she would never make the same mistakes.

The memory helped. Suddenly she felt a lot stronger.

She stood up and put on her jacket, ran a smoothing hand over her hair, checked her reflection in the mirror by the door and then picked up her papers. She could do this.

Most of the board were already seated when she walked into the room, but there were a couple of places vacant, and she slipped into the one furthest away from Alexi.

He was seated at the head of the long, polished table and her eyes collided with his as she looked over. Immediately she looked away again. Best not to make eye-contact, she told herself, best just to look at her work, or at anyone else but him! Otherwise she was going to sound like a gibbering idiot when she made her presentation.

The last of the board members arrived, and Alexi called for order. Immediately a hush fell over the proceedings.

'Gentlemen, I'm very glad so many of you have been able to make our meeting today, as it was called at short notice. I would like to start by welcoming our new project manager, Ms Katie Connor, into our midst. I'm sure she will be a valued member of the team, and I look forward to a close and harmonious working relationship.'

Katie's eyes clashed with his again, and she felt her nerves jangle. She wasn't looking forward to any such thing—well, not with *him* at any rate! Hurriedly she looked away and tried to concentrate as he introduced the people around the table to her.

He probably wouldn't be around much, she told herself again soothingly as she smiled in acknowledgement to the few people who spoke to her. He'd be at his head office here in London or in New York, or maybe his office in Athens…

'Perhaps you would like to proceed, Katie?' he invited smoothly. 'Run us through your findings.'

'Thank you.' She forced herself to smile coolly at him as she got to her feet. This was horrible—truly horrible. But she had to be businesslike and focus her attention away from him, she told herself firmly.

Alexi sat back and watched her with interest. She gave a very confident performance, running through her assessment of the company's position within the holiday market, running through her proposals for increasing their slice of that market. She'd obviously done a lot of research before starting work here today. No wonder she had been so shocked to see him. He'd managed to keep his ownership of the company out of the financial news so far, mainly because he'd wanted to be one step ahead of his competitors, but it was an added bonus that he'd managed to snare Katie back into working for him in the process. He'd wanted her for this job all along—he'd known she would be perfect for it.

For a moment his eyes slipped down over her body.

OK, that wasn't all he wanted; he acknowledged the truth as he felt the sudden fierce pull of attraction for her. She had a fantastic figure, and he remembered all too well how much he had enjoyed exploring those sensational curves. Beneath that strait-laced exterior he had found her to be hot and passionate, and he had wanted her from the first moment she had looked at him with those innocently come-hither, violet-blue eyes.

And he still wanted her now.

That fact was eating him away. It was crazy—there were other beautiful women he could replace her with, women who were only too eager for him. Why did Katie haunt his thoughts? Why, from the first moment when she'd told him it was over, had he wanted her back? It wasn't like him. Since his divorce eight years ago he hadn't got emotionally tied up with anyone. Nor did he plan to— he would *never* get serious about a woman again.

Yet he hadn't wanted to let Katie go. He'd had to force

himself to walk away and continue as normal. And despite the fact that he'd been gaining control of two new companies, and had been up to his neck in work, she'd been on his mind morning, noon and night…especially night.

The answer had come to him today when he'd looked at her again. She'd haunted him because she'd dented his ego; it was as simple as that. Usually he was the one who ended relationships; he was used to calling the shots. As soon as things started to get complicated or he'd had his fill of someone he moved on. But Katie had ended things before he was ready. They had unfinished business. It was called *lust*.

It was a relief to finally know why she had unsettled him so much. And there was an easy remedy for lust. All he had to do was get her back into his bed again and take his fill of her.

She looked over at him at that moment, and he smiled. Then he watched the blaze of fire in her eyes, noted the way her skin heated up as she moved her attention away.

She wasn't as coldly indifferent to him as she acted. It shouldn't be too difficult to have her back on his terms, he told himself confidently. Acquisitions had always been his strong point. And this time he would be the one to finish things.

'So, has anyone got any questions?' she asked briskly.

As he'd predicted a few members of the board gave her a tough time, started to grill her more intensely, but she more than held her own. After a few more minutes he could see that there was a shifting change of attitude and she was winning them over.

'Well, I think you have just about covered everything, Katie, thank you,' he said smoothly.

She nodded and started to close her notes. 'Then, if you'll excuse me, I'll leave you to the rest of your meeting, gentlemen, and I'll press on.'

'Certainly.'

Relief coursed through her. She couldn't wait to get out of here.

'Just one last thing,' Alexi added nonchalantly. 'There is another meeting at the office in New York tomorrow, and I will need you to attend.'

She looked up and he held her eyes.

'Tomorrow?' Apprehension clutched at her stomach. 'That's rather short notice, isn't it?'

'One of those things.' Alexi shrugged.

'What time is the meeting?' She wrenched her gaze away from him, picked up her pen and looked back at her notepad.

'No need to sort flights; you can come with me on the company jet later.'

Katie's head jerked up. She felt like she was already on that plane and it had just dropped into free fall from thirty-five-thousand feet. Her whole body was telling her that being alone with him for hours was not a good idea! She wanted to say, *no way*, but how unprofessional would that look?

'I think it would be sensible to sort things out in the USA as soon as possible,' Alexi continued coolly.

A few of the people around the table were starting their own conversations now, and under cover of the sudden babble of noise she wanted to lower her voice and tell him that she didn't think it was a sensible idea at all. That she didn't want to be alone with him—that she couldn't handle this situation, *couldn't act as if nothing had happened between them!*

But she didn't say any of those things—she had her

pride. Instead her eyes remained locked with his, and her heart thundered so hard that it felt like it might break out of her chest. 'I suppose so.' She said the words tightly.

'Good. I'll pick you up at seven this evening.'

Was it her imagination or was there a gleam of triumph in those dark eyes?

She looked away from him and picked up her notes with hands that were not entirely steady.

'I'll see you later.' What else could she say or do? she wondered furiously. This was about work. He had her in an impossible situation.

CHAPTER THREE

IT WAS almost seven in the evening, and Katie was pacing her apartment. Her weekend case was packed, and the professional side of her was ready to go—but emotionally she was reluctant.

In fact when Alexi had rung her at her desk earlier, to confirm flight times and the time for picking her up, she'd tried her best to get out of it.

'Is this trip really necessary so soon?' she'd demanded heatedly. 'Don't you think it would be better for me to get to grips with the job here and get on top of a lot of this paperwork before sorting out the US side of things?'

'You can sort some of the paperwork out on the flight. I need to press ahead as fast as possible with this,' he'd answered without hesitation. 'So be ready and waiting for me.'

Then the line had just gone dead. He'd hung up on her.

The nerve of the guy! OK, he was her boss—but that didn't mean he owned her twenty-four-seven. He at least owed her the courtesy of some advance warning!

Her mobile phone zinged with a message now as she tried to pull herself together. She took it out of her pocket and opened it. It was from Alexi. It was strange, seeing his name on the screen after all this time. She'd thought he'd probably deleted her number from his phone weeks ago. She'd certainly meant to delete his, she'd just… Well, she hadn't got round to it.

Quickly she read the message: *I'm outside—don't be long.* Anger twisted inside her. Four weeks of nothing and then a curt summons. Then she bit down on her lip and reminded herself that this was about work, nothing else. She couldn't let emotions cloud the issue.

She went across to the window and looked out, and sure enough his limousine was sitting next to the kerb. Just the sight of it made her heartbeat start to accelerate. She had a choice—she could either forget this job and tell him to go to hell, or she could put work first and get on with it. When she thought about it like that she didn't really have a choice, she told herself wryly. Her job and her independence were the most important things to her, and she'd always acted in a professional manner. She snapped up her jacket and her bag and headed for the door. She wasn't going to allow herself to be preoccupied by something that had happened in the past. She had to put work first.

Alexi had just taken his phone out to ring her when she appeared on the street. He smiled to himself and put the mobile away again. Things were going extremely well. Businesswise, he had Katie exactly where he wanted her, and before they returned to London he would have her back in his bed as well. He watched as his driver got out to help her with her bag and to open the door for her.

'Hi.' She acknowledged him with a nod as she slid into the seat opposite. He could smell the familiar scent of her perfume, flowery and light, and yet somehow incredibly sexy. She was wearing black jeans with a white shirt, and she had tied her hair back from her face. She looked good. Possibly too good, considering the fact that he had to get some work done during this journey.

'You're late,' he told her sardonically.

'I was five minutes!' Her beautiful blue eyes seemed to simmer. 'And you're lucky I'm here at all. This is very short notice, I could have had other plans.'

'But you don't,' he concluded.

'That's not the point. I really need at least a few days' notice for business trips away like this.'

'I'll bear that in mind for the next time.'

'The next time?' She sounded suddenly flustered. 'Do you think we will have to make many more trips like this?'

He inclined his head. 'Definitely. We'll need to iron out as many teething problems up front as possible, and there is no better way than the personal touch.'

'I see.' She looked away from him, out of the windows.

What was causing that flutter of panic? he wondered. It couldn't be work—she was well used to travelling between different offices; she'd done it at Demetri Shipping. Was it the thought of being alone with him?

What had made her finish things with him? he wondered angrily. She had always been passionately compliant and eager for his kisses…what had changed that?

The briefcase she had placed next to her on the seat fell over as the car made a U-turn at a junction. Alexi reached to catch it at the same time as Katie, and for just a second their hands touched on the leather strap.

She pulled away as if she had been burnt, allowing him to place it safely back beside her.

'Thanks.' She could barely look at him now.

'Everything OK, Katie?' he enquired casually.

'Of course.' She glanced at him, but there was a blush over the high cheekbones that said differently and her eyes were over-bright.

If he could make her skin heat up with just the brush of his fingertips, make her eyes sparkle with fire, what would happen if he *really* touched her? In the past it had always been spontaneous combustion.

He itched to find out now if the old magic was still there. He wanted to lean forward and take hold of her hand, find her lips and devour her.

His eyes moved to the buttons on her blouse. He imagined himself unbuttoning them; he remembered how firm and willing her body had been.

With difficulty he forced himself to sit back against the comfortable leather seat and bide his time. The chase was on, but he couldn't rush it. When he took Katie again he wanted her to be wild for him…desperate for him. He was going to make her want him so badly she wouldn't know what day it was.

'Did you get the paperwork we need to sort out?' he asked casually.

'Yes, I brought it with me—it isn't finished, obviously, but…' She started to unzip her bag.

'We'll go through it on the plane.'

'Oh! OK.' She fastened the bag back up.

Silence stretched between them. Her eyes darted over to him. He looked powerfully dynamic in the dark business-suit, every inch the successful business-tycoon. For a moment it was hard to believe that he had once been her lover, that he had once held her so tenderly, made love to her so passionately. He looked over at her and her eyes veered hurriedly away again. Thoughts like that were not helping her!

'So how have things been with you, Katie?'

The sudden personal question made her look back at him warily. 'Absolutely fine—why do you ask?'

There was a glimmer of amusement in the darkness of his eyes now. 'Because I'm interested to know how you are; what other reason would there be?'

'I don't know.' She shrugged and forced herself to try and relax. But the confined space and the memories he conjured up were sending her blood pressure soaring. Even the touch of his fingertips against her hand a few moments ago had sent her senses into a spin. 'Let's face it. You've never been one for making small talk, Alexi.'

'Haven't I?' He shrugged. 'I'm sure we had our moments.'

She kept her composure with difficulty. She really didn't want to think about what moments he might be referring to—not now.

'It wasn't all work between us—there was quite a bit of play time,' he continued nonchalantly.

Her eyes snapped with sudden fire. 'I really don't think we should be discussing that!'

'Don't you?'

She allowed her eyes to hold firmly with his. 'We've moved on, remember?'

'Ah, yes.'

His gaze flicked down towards her lips and she found herself remembering the way he could kiss her and caress her and make her feel truly alive.

The intensity of the memory stirred up a painful need inside her, and she wrenched her eyes away from him and looked out of the window again. She needed to forget the past. He wasn't the type of man to get serious about; they'd had their fun. It was over.

'But it's good that we can move on and work together, without any discord, don't you think?' he said smoothly.

'Yes, of course.'

He noticed that her hands had curled into tight fists at her side, and he smiled.

'So, tell me, what have you been doing with yourself since you moved on?' he invited conversationally.

She shrugged and tried desperately to just treat him like any other work colleague. 'I went to visit my sister in France for a week.'

'I didn't know you had a sister.'

'Didn't you?' She couldn't stop herself from flicking him a pointed look. 'Perhaps because our conversations always revolved around work; in fact, you don't know a lot about me at all.'

Something about the way she said that struck a cord in him. To a certain extent she was right; he'd tended to focus on their work connection more than anything else. He didn't do deep and meaningful; he'd been happy with the equation the way it was—but so had she. He'd noticed on more than one occasion that she'd used work to hide behind.

He'd noticed the way she had looked sometimes—the unguarded vulnerability in her eyes when she thought he wasn't watching her. 'I know that when we met you'd been hurt by some guy in the past.'

The observation took her by surprise. She had mentioned Carl once very briefly at the start of their relationship—but she hadn't thought he was paying that much attention.

'Now, what was it you said…?' He frowned. 'Ah…I know. You said you'd been in a serious relationship and had had enough hearts and flowers, and that sex and straight talking would do nicely instead.'

Katie looked at him in consternation. She couldn't believe she had said that—but she had, the first time he'd taken her to bed. It had felt so good in his arms, and afterwards when he had reiterated something about 'not doing hearts and flowers' she'd made that glib reply.

'Trust you to remember that!' she murmured with acute embarrassment. 'But you can't remember I have a sister!'

He gave her a teasing look that made her want to melt inside. With difficulty she zoned out from the feeling. Melting around Alexi wasn't recommended.

Alexi smiled. 'By the way, remind me later to look out the figures we were discussing at the meeting this morning,' he remarked casually as he glanced at his watch. 'We need to fine-hone any problems with the timetable.'

She'd almost forgotten the way he was always able to switch back to business at a snap. How one moment he could play the consummate, arousing lover and the next the steel shutters of his mind could come crashing down to the focus of his real agenda, the real heart of his life: business.

'Yes, of course.' She nodded and tried to make herself sound as cool as he did.

They were arriving at the airport. She noticed that the warm June evening looked grey and wintry through the tinted glass. Amazing how your senses could be deceived by an illusion.

She'd deluded herself into thinking she could handle an affair with Alexi. The truth was she had been ensnared by that mesmerising way he had of turning her on with just a look, and she'd started to read things into it that hadn't been there. He'd never lied to her, he'd never told her that she was special or led her on in any way—yet his kisses and his love-making had done the lying for him. Being with him had been somehow addictive, and to get her fix she had reassured herself that her emotions were not in any way involved, hence those glib remarks when she had first slept with him. But the truth was she had found it harder and harder to disconnect her feelings.

She bit down on her lip as she admitted the full extent of her mistake. Some sort of madness must have possessed her. Or maybe on a subconscious level she'd lied to herself as self-preservation against getting involved with someone who was clearly a heartbreaker.

At least she had pulled herself back from the brink before any *real* disaster. And she had to differentiate between what was real and what was an illusion now.

Alexi the steely controlled businessman was real— Alexi the warm, passionate lover was not.

The car pulled to a halt by the edge of the airfield and the driver came round and opened the door for them. Katie stepped out into the warmth of the evening. The company jet was standing on the tarmac ready and waiting for them with the steps down.

Someone came over to speak to Alexi. There were a few formalities, and moments later they were proceeding up the steps into the luxury of the aircraft.

Katie had travelled on board the aeroplane with Alexi just once before when they'd been attending a conference in Paris. She didn't want to think about how they'd spent that one-hour flight now. It was definitely better forgotten when she had hours alone with him stretching ahead.

She took some papers out of her briefcase and put them on the seat beside her before placing the case in the overhead compartment. Then she sat next to the window and fastened her seatbelt.

Alexi was talking to the pilot. The door was open between the cabin and the cockpit, and Katie tried to pretend that she had been focusing on the dials and lights of the controls rather than on Alexi as he turned towards her.

He was too damn handsome, she thought distractedly. At thirty-five, he was definitely a man in his prime. The suit sat perfectly on his broad-shouldered frame, the white shirt emphasising the olive tones of his skin, the darkness of his hair and eyes.

He took the suit jacket off and tossed it casually over the arm of the seat before putting his case overhead. There wasn't a spare inch of flesh on him; he was lean and muscular and incredibly fit. She wrenched her eyes away as he took the seat opposite.

'We should have a smooth flight; the weather forecast is good,' he told her as he fastened his seatbelt.

One less thing to worry about then, she thought dryly. Now if she could just keep her mind on work and not on how attractive she found him, and how pleasurable that hour had been in here last time, she'd be OK.

He smiled at her. 'We'll get through some of that paperwork as soon as we take off. Then hopefully there will be time to relax, get some sleep.'

She remembered him telling her that these huge seats folded down into beds. However they had never actually got round to converting the seats, they'd been in too much of a hurry. They'd just folded down the armrests, and then Alexi had reached for her...

Her stomach dipped with a sudden surge of adrenalin. *Don't think about it*, she warned herself fiercely.

The door between them and the pilot closed, sealing them in alone. Then the engines fired up and after a few moments they were taxiing out along the runway. She glanced out of the window. Dusk was falling fast. Night flights were good, she told herself positively. After the day she'd had, she would probably have no difficulty sleeping.

They halted at the start of the runway as they waited for take-off clearance.

Her eyes met with Alexi.

'Do you remember our flight to Paris?' he asked her suddenly.

She felt that dipping sensation in her stomach again. 'No. Not really.'

He smiled, and she realised her reply didn't fool him for a moment.

'And I'm surprised you remember it,' she continued swiftly. 'I mean, one dalliance at thirty-five-thousand feet must be like another to you.'

One eyebrow rose at that. 'You think?'

She shrugged and looked away from him.

He said something to her in Greek suddenly. Although his looks were Mediterranean, it always surprised her to hear him speak his native language, possibly because he spoke such perfect English.

'What does that mean?' she asked him, trying to ignore how the sound of his voice sent provocative shivers racing through her.

'It means that I thought our time together that day was pretty spectacular.' He laughed as she flushed a deep shade of beetroot. 'And I'm glad now that I didn't tell you the exact translation—otherwise you might set the cabin on fire.'

'Stop it, Alexi!' she muttered in embarrassment. 'The past is forgotten, OK? It's a taboo subject—a different planet.'

He shot her a mocking look as the aircraft-engines

roared, and suddenly they were thundering down the runway. 'Time for take off.'

He seemed to be taking a perverse pleasure in deliberately winding her up, she thought uncomfortably.

How was she going to get through this time alone with him?

She didn't think she would ever be able to be at ease with him again. It was too...dangerous. He'd made her behave in a way that was totally out of character for her. Made her desire him...and need him. She didn't want to remember that. But being around him made it almost impossible to forget.

The plane lifted off the ground, and for a moment there was a weightless sensation as they floated up through the clouds.

The lights of London disappeared, and a little while later the seatbelt sign was switched off.

'Do you want a drink before we get down to things?' He glanced over.

'No thanks.' Even the way he was wording things was sending her nervous system into orbit. Everything was going to be OK, she told herself steadily, as long as she kept her senses firmly in the land of reality and the present.

Alexi got to his feet to take out his briefcase from the overhead compartment. 'So, you didn't tell me—what part of France does your sister live in?' he asked idly as he snapped it open and took papers out.

'The southwest; a small village called Aviger.'

'Is she married to a Frenchman?'

'No, Lucy is single.'

Her sister was as bad at picking men as she was, Katie thought wryly. In fact they had both decided not long ago that it was the curse of the Connor family. Her mother's bad choices in men were legendary, and they had suffered considerably in childhood as a consequence. They'd been dragged from one bad situation to the next. No wonder they were both wary of giving their hearts, and both fiercely independent.

Katie had always been determined not to be like her mother. When she had got involved with Carl she had done so believing him to be the steady, dependable type. It had been ages before she had invited him into her bed. She'd wanted to be sure about him.

But how could you be sure about anybody? It had turned out that he had just seen her as a challenge. Once he'd taken her to bed and the thrill of the chase had gone, he'd been ready to move on to the next conquest.

Life was one big learning curve, she thought now as she looked across at Alexi. And she didn't want to learn anything more about heartache.

'We need to get on with those timetables.' She changed the subject swiftly away from the personal angle. She needed to take her lead from Alexi and be motivated solely by business. 'And I've been thinking about what plans we could incorporate to make the strategy for increasing business greener.'

'Have you, now?'

'Yes, and I have a few ideas that I think we should explore.'

'I'm remembering now why I wanted you for this job.'

Was he being facetious, or was he just thinking about work? It was hard to tell.

The colour in her skin heightened slightly, but she continued on, her voice brisk and determined. He watched as she picked up the papers she had left on the seat beside her.

He noticed the way she bit down on her lower lip as she scanned through the pages.

He'd forgotten that she did that when she was trying to focus. Forgotten how businesslike she could sound, and yet how vulnerable she could look. How confident and grown up she could act and yet how lost she could seem.

There was something almost innocent about her. He remembered thinking that the first time he'd taken her to bed. Despite her glib words about being happy with a no-strings affair, he'd always suspected she'd spoken the words to mask a bruised heart.

She hadn't been a virgin, but she'd been untutored in the art of love-making. She'd been almost tentatively afraid of giving herself to him, yet at the same time eager and willing for his kiss, his touch.

He'd found the combination explosive, had enjoyed drawing her out, teaching her how to please him.

Just thinking about it now made him want her all the more.

She looked up at him and he forced himself to concentrate on what she was saying. Work had to come first.

However, one thing was clear—he couldn't wait too long before taking her to his bed again; his body was getting impatient. He felt edgy with need. And that was a situation he was very unused to.

CHAPTER FOUR

WHEN Katie opened her eyes and glanced out of the aircraft window she could see the lights of Manhattan shimmering against the darkness of the sky.

'We'll be touching down in twenty minutes,' Alexi told her as he packed away the papers he'd been working on.

She must have fallen asleep, she realised with a start. How had she managed that when he'd been sitting opposite her working all night? She'd been determined not to give in to the overwhelming waves of tiredness—even when Alexi had told her to put her work away and make the seat into a bed she had resolutely refused. She hadn't wanted to let her guard down around him for even one minute, had wanted to remain confident and poised. Now look at her! She self-consciously put a hand up to her hair, trying to smooth back the long, silky strands that had escaped to curl around her face. She felt a complete wreck.

Her eyes connected with Alexi's across the narrow divide, and she felt the tension that had twisted between them all night flare instantly into life again.

'Gosh, I didn't mean to fall asleep,' she murmured. 'Did you finish the timetable?'

'Yes, it's all in order. You probably should have got your head down properly. I hope you can function at our meeting.'

The cool words irritated her. Typical that he should only be worried about the business that lay ahead and not about her welfare!

'If you can function, then I'm damn sure I can,' she murmured.

Her sparkly determination made him smile, and for a moment he allowed his eyes to slip over her. She'd been curled up like a kitten within stroking distance, and she had been driving him out of his mind—so much so that he'd had to ban himself from looking at her, because no work had been done whilst he'd been drinking her in like a mind-altering drug.

The smooth perfection of her skin had fascinated him, as had the long, thick darkness of her lashes, the soft curve of her lips. He even liked the messed-up way her hair was curling around her face. It was saucy and sexy, and that was before his eyes had travelled downwards to her sumptuous curves.

With difficulty he concentrated his gaze upwards and noticed suddenly that she seemed very pale.

Katie looked away from him and tried to concentrate on something other than the wave of nausea that had unexpectedly swept over her. What on earth was the matter with her? She couldn't be ill, not here. Not in front of him! How embarrassing would that be? Panic-stricken, she took a few deep breaths, and to her relief the feeling started to subside. She was just tired, she told herself soothingly. Apart from the hour's sleep, she'd been almost permanently on the go for the last twenty-four. A new job, a high-pressured meeting followed by piles of paperwork and then a flight to New York—all that plus Alexi. No wonder she didn't feel well!

And the time spent working with Alexi had been difficult, to say the least. After the initial conversation, they'd hardly exchanged a word that wasn't connected with what they were doing. The ease with which they had once worked together had definitely gone.

Katie tried to tell herself that the worst was behind her now. A long, refreshing shower and a sleep in a comfortable bed for a few hours would probably sort her out.

She looked at her wristwatch and adjusted the time back five hours to New York time. It was like that film *Groundhog Day*, she thought; just when you thought the long hours of darkness were nearly over, it was back to the small hours of the morning.

She glanced over and found Alexi still watching her. 'What time is our meeting?' she asked awkwardly.

'Nine-thirty. So we'll have time to get to my apartment and catch some sleep.'

'Your apartment?' She tried to make her voice light. 'I assumed we would be staying at a hotel!' *Preferably with rooms on different floors*, she thought frantically.

'No, I have an apartment by Central Park. It's very convenient.'

The jet was making its final descent, the engine noises screaming a bit like her nerves. But at least it covered the tense silence that now lay between them. She closed her eyes and tried to pretend she was somewhere else—anywhere else but here with him.

But instead of thinking relaxing, comforting thoughts her mind was now racing over the fact that they were going to be alone in an apartment.

The plane touched down on the runway with a heavy thud and a screech of brakes. As it taxied to a halt, they started to gather their belongings, ready to disembark.

'You know, Alexi, I really think I should stay at a hotel,' she said suddenly.

He looked amused. 'Why?'

'Because...I feel this is an awkward situation, that's why.'

'My apartment has more than one bedroom, Katie.'

'It's not that,' she said heatedly.

'No?' He looked over at her with a raised eyebrow. 'Then what is it? Are you frightened you can't be alone with me without wanting to return to my bed?' The teasingly arrogant question created a tidal wave of anger and consternation inside of her.

'Of course I'm not worried about that!' Her voice rose slightly. 'I haven't even given such a thing a second thought!'

'Well, I can't see your problem, then.' Alexi put on his jacket. 'Did you make a note about the new environmental data, by the way?'

The swift return to their earlier discussion threw her. 'Yes, of course.'

'Good. When we get to the meeting this morning, we can go over the ideas. I think they will be well received.' Alexi passed her the briefcase that she had placed in the overhead locker.

'I'm sure they will.' Desperately she tried to refocus her mind. She didn't want to make too much of an issue about the apartment now, didn't want him to think she was in any way frightened that she might weaken and go back into his arms. The conceited audacity of the question was still burning inside her. Or was it the fact that deep down she knew he was right? And she wasn't just frightened, she was *terrified*!

When it came to Alexi she had a weakness—she acted first and thought later. It was a highly unusual mode of behaviour for her, but she had to be honest with herself: it was what had happened before, and she couldn't let it happen again!

What she needed was to get out of this situation as soon as possible. 'When are we flying back to London?' she asked abruptly.

He flicked her an impatient look. 'Possibly tomorrow; it depends on how these two meetings go.'

The door of the plane opened and he led the way out.

'I thought there was just one meeting?' Katie asked as she struggled to keep up with his long strides down towards immigration control.

'No, there are two. The first and most important is at my main office in town. But there is a second one down at the docks later this afternoon. My ship, the *Octavia*, is moored here and the accountants will be on board. We're in conference at three.'

'I see. Well, that should be straightforward enough. We could fly back tonight.'

'Except that I have to attend a champagne party tonight, which is also on board the *Octavia*.' He glanced over at her. 'I want you to tag along to that,' he added casually. 'It will be a chance for you to get to know a few people socially.'

'You didn't tell me there would be a party!' The last thing she wanted was to attend a social function with him! 'I haven't brought anything to wear!'

'Don't worry, you can pick something up at one of the boutiques on board this afternoon. It's no big deal.'

He made it sound all very logical, very relaxed. But to her this was a nostalgic tug of remembrance. She'd attended one of these parties in the past on one of his cruise liners docked at Southampton. It had been a very enjoyable occasion; she'd loved indulging in a glass of champagne and socialising with Alexi. Although she had been there in a work capacity, and she'd had to write up a report afterwards, it hadn't felt like work. Later when everyone had left she'd danced with Alexi under the stars, and he had held her close in his arms.

'You better not put this in your report,' he'd murmured as he slid the zip of her dress down.

The memory made her body tense.

She needed to avoid anything remotely approaching a social occasion with him, because it felt like perilous territory. In fact the whole damn trip now felt like a minefield.

Before she could say anything, however, they were next in line for the formalities of Immigration, and then they were outside and getting into Alexi's waiting limousine.

'That didn't take too long.' Alexi glanced at his watch. 'We should have time to get a few hours in bed.'

Katie looked away from him, out at the sparkling skyline of Manhattan.

Just over a month ago she would have enjoyed a few hours in bed with Alexi. And she would have been excited about being here; she'd never visited New York before. She'd have been hoping they could get away from work to see the sights—she would have been looking forward to spending time alone with him, going into his arms, cuddling in next to his powerful body...

But that was when she had foolishly thought she could handle a no-strings affair, she reminded herself quickly. And she knew differently now.

Alexi's mobile rang and he spent the remainder of the

journey talking to someone in London about a staffing solution he was putting together for Tellesta's international chain of shops.

This was the reality of being with Alexi, she reminded herself. All his time was utilised; even when they'd been having an affair their love-making had been slotted in around the important deals.

They were gliding down through a mid-town tunnel now, and then a little while later Katie was craning her head, looking up at the skyscrapers towering over them.

Suddenly they were on Fifth Avenue. Katie recognised shops and names that she had only ever seen on the pages of glossy magazines and in the films. The limousine rounded a corner and pulled up outside an impressive building that was glass-fronted.

'I'll phone you back later today, Harry, when the offices are open.' Alexi ended his call as the driver got out to open the door for them.

Instantly the sounds of the city spilled in. Despite the fact that it was the early hours, still the traffic was constant. There was a smell of tar and road fumes.

For a moment it made Katie feel distinctly queasy again.

She followed Alexi along the strip of red carpet that ran up the steps into the building. A doorman tipped his hat at them and swung the heavy glass doors open.

Then they stepped into a waiting lift in the marble foyer and were swept upwards.

Neither spoke, but Katie was aware of Alexi's eyes on her. She wondered what he was thinking.

She wondered if he had a new girlfriend in his life now. As soon as the question occurred to her, she berated herself severely. It was a month since their affair had ended, and

Alexi probably wouldn't even have waited a day before replacing her in his bed.

No doubt he was dating some stunning model or debutante now.

Katie, on the other hand, hadn't even looked at another man. But she would soon, she reassured herself firmly. And in the meantime whoever Alexi was dating was welcome to him, because like all the others she wouldn't last.

'You look a little pale, Katie.'

The sudden remark took her by surprise. 'Do I? It's probably these overhead lights.'

Alexi nodded.

For a second their eyes connected, and immediately she wished that they hadn't. He had the sexiest eyes on the planet: dark, bold come-to-bed eyes that seemed to sear her to the very bone.

The lift jolted to a stop and the doors slid open. Alexi led the way towards a doorway opposite.

A turn of a key, and Katie stepped into a luxurious apartment with wide windows facing out towards Central Park.

'Make a coffee, will you, whilst I check my emails?' Alexi ordered casually as he tossed his keys down on a table and turned on some lights.

So much for his caring, 'you look a little pale' moment, she thought sardonically. This was more like it. She put her overnight bag down on a chair and walked over towards the open-plan kitchen to fill the kettle.

The place was very stylish, solid-oak floors and minimalist furniture. 'Did you get the same person to design this as your London apartment?' she asked casually as she found some cups.

Alexi didn't answer her, and she glanced over to find

that she was on her own; he'd disappeared through the doorway at the end of the corridor.

She followed him a few moments later with a steaming cup of freshly ground coffee, and found him in a small office adjoining one of the bedrooms.

'One black coffee, no sugar.' She put it down next to him, and then stood watching whilst he sorted through some papers he'd taken from his briefcase.

'Thanks, Katie, did we get the codes for the files we need today?' he asked without looking up.

'Yes, I put them with the forms I filled out earlier.'

'Great. You can turn in now if you want.'

'Thanks,' she murmured dryly. 'Which room can I have?'

'Which room do you want?' He looked up at her suddenly, a flare of teasing light in the darkness of his eyes. 'Mine is the one at the end of the corridor. You can take your pick.'

The memory of his earlier, arrogant comment trickled through her.

'Well, any room but that, then.' She tried to sound flippant.

He smiled as if he found her the most amusing woman he'd ever met. 'If that's what you want.'

'Of course it's what I want.' Her heart missed a beat as he started to get up from behind the desk. Suddenly she could feel alarm bells ringing with piercing intensity.

'Katie, I think we've known each other long enough for you to be able to drop this pretence…don't you?'

'I don't know what you are talking about! I'm not pretending about anything!' She swallowed hard.

'No?' He looked relaxed as he leaned back against the desk and fixed her with a probing look. 'I think you are. I think the fact that there is still a chemistry buzzing between us is driving you out of your mind.'

He was so damn sure of himself that it was galling! 'I honestly don't know what you are talking about!' She did the only thing she could; she lied vehemently. It was either that or she would lose her self-respect along with her defences.

'Don't you?' His lips curved in a sardonic smile. 'So, why the panicky look?'

'I'm not panicky...' The lie was so great it was almost laughable, and he obviously wasn't in the slightest bit fooled because he smiled.

'Honey, we are going to have to address this.'

'I'm not your *honey*, and there is nothing to address!' She was suddenly furious, but more with herself than with him, because he was so right. How was she going to work with him when she felt like this? She made to move past him, but he reached out and caught hold of her arm, stopping her.

'Katie, let's not lie to each other, hmm?' He said the words softly. 'We've never lied to each other, have we?'

'You're right, the one thing we had was honesty.' She looked up at him, her eyes flashing fire. 'We both knew from day one that what we had together wasn't going to last beyond the end of my contract with Demetri Shipping.' Her voice trembled slightly as she strove to pull herself together.

'But it has lasted.' He said the words huskily and turned her towards him forcefully. 'Against the odds, I'll grant you. The chemistry is alive and well...'

She shook her head, but he reached out and tipped her chin upwards, forcing her to look up at him.

The touch of his fingers against her skin was intensely disturbing, and for all the wrong reasons. She wanted him to deepen the touch...wanted him to stroke his hand through her hair, lower his head, claim her mouth and take possession of her. The need was like a palpable ache inside her. And she hated herself for it.

'In fact, the chemistry is even stronger than it once was,' he told her softly. 'And the memory of how good sex was between us is there every time our eyes meet. It was there in the office yesterday, on the journey last night, even in the lift just now…'

'That's an outrageous thing to say!' To her distress, her voice shook.

'Probably, but it's still the truth.' He smiled. 'It's the elephant in the room. It's with us now. And trying to pretend otherwise isn't working.'

She wanted to contest that, but the touch of his hand against her skin was throwing her senses into chaos. How could she deny it when the need for him was eating away at her, when she longed to feel his body closer, his lips on hers?

'So, the question is, what should we do about it?' he continued huskily.

The question punched through her. 'We're not going to do anything about it, Alexi.' Her voice trembled alarmingly now. 'We both know that the kind of relationship we had is transitory—you move on and you don't go back.'

His eyes were on her lips. 'But you don't move on until the music has stopped. It's a dance, Katie…' He paused. 'Unless you have met someone else. Is that what this is about?' He forced himself to ask the question, his eyes watchful, his manner still.

'No!' Her eyes locked with his. She couldn't lie to him. 'That's not what this is about.'

He smiled.

'I just don't want you to call the tune any more!' she murmured huskily.

'But you still want me, Katie. I can see it now in the way you look at me.'

She felt a shudder of ecstasy race straight through her body as his hand softly stroked along the column of her neck.

'In fact you want me to just *take you* right now.' He leaned forward and whispered the words against her ear.

His close proximity was so sweet it was tormenting. He was right. She did want that. No one could make her feel the way he could. The memory of how good things had been between them played enticingly through her.

He watched as she moistened her lips, saw the way her eyes deepened to an almost sultry, smoky violet. 'Don't do this, Alexi,' she whispered breathlessly.

'Do what...tell the truth?' He smiled.

'Hell, but you are so very conceited.' She murmured the words, totally flustered. 'Conceited and arrogant, and—'

'So if I were to kiss you now for old times' sake you wouldn't enjoy it in the slightest?'

He was rewarded by the flush of heat across her cheekbones and the flare of light in her blue eyes. 'You see? You are a long way from being indifferent towards me, Katie.' His eyes flicked down over the curves of her body, noting the rapid rise and fall of her chest. 'And the chemistry is a long, *long* way from finished.'

As if to demonstrate his power over her, his hands moved possessively to her waist, drawing her closer. His hand cupped her slender body, his fingers splayed over her ribcage, and immediately her body tingled with pleasure. She wanted to feel the touch of his hands moving higher, her breasts felt taut with the desire for his caress...

His gaze raked over her with an almost ruthless intent,

and he smiled as he saw the stark hunger in the deep violet-blue of her eyes. 'We both know that this is inevitable.'

'Alexi, please…' She whispered the words rawly.

'Please *what*…?' He smiled and his hands brushed upwards, stroking over the curve of her breast with a possessive touch that made her gasp with need.

'Please *what*…?' He taunted again softly, but his voice wasn't entirely free from desire. It grated unevenly with the force of need.

And somehow the fact that momentarily he was as much lost in desire as she was made her defences start to crumble.

'Alexi…' Her voice broke slightly as she turned her lips instinctively towards his and kissed him.

He felt a powerful surge of triumph, and for a moment allowed her the first tentative moments of the kiss, tasting her submission, her need. *She did want him—he knew it!* And then he took control, plundering her mouth with hard, possessive lips. How he'd held back even for a moment he didn't know because now he'd taken over he didn't want to stop kissing her. He wanted her with a driving, forceful need he didn't think he had ever experienced before. It shook him senseless. It also angered him. He was a man who needed no one—who could take a woman or leave a woman without a care. What was it about Katie that made him feel like this? He didn't want to feel like this. However, that rage just seemed to fuel his desire even more.

She reached up and allowed her arms to wind around his neck, allowed her senses to capitulate and breathe him in, to respond wildly. Would it be so wrong to go to bed with him one last time? The words sizzled through her consciousness.

She'd missed him so much…she needed him so much.

The papers on the desk behind them were swept to the floor as he pressed her back against the desk. Then he dragged his lips away from hers and started to unbutton her blouse.

She wanted him so much that she couldn't stop him, but deep inside there was another emotion swirling with desire, and that was fear: fear because she wanted him too much. She didn't want to need any man, let alone someone as unsuitable as Alexi. She didn't want to be just used for sex and discarded!

'We shouldn't do this,' she whispered as he unfastened her jeans.

'Why not?' His hands slid over the narrow curve of her waist, then stroked down lower over the flat plane of her stomach.

'Because it's just sex.' She forced herself to say the words. 'It means nothing,' she whispered fiercely. 'Nothing.'

His dark eyes blazed into hers for a second. 'It doesn't have to mean something to be addictive. We both know that.'

The words shouldn't have hurt her...but they did. 'We should stop!' she whispered softly. 'Before this goes too far!'

The tremulous words made him pull back from her slightly, made him try to contain his need. But it was like trying to pull back from the force of gravity. It took all his control.

What kind of game was she playing? he wondered suddenly. Was she just a teasing little witch who knew how she affected him and played it for all it was worth? Well, no woman would ever have control over him like that again! The furious fire of need glimmered white-hot inside him now. He was taking control; he would decide when this was finished...not her.

'But that's not really what you want, is it, Katie?' he

grated. 'You'd hate me to stop, because you want this…'
As he spoke his hand moved lower, pushing the flimsy
pants she wore to one side and finding the core of her with
an unerring accuracy that made her body tingle with
pleasure.

He was right; she didn't want him to stop. She closed
her eyes as a wave of ecstasy shot through her. How did
he know how to do that? How could he pleasure her with
just the lightest touch…?

Then he stopped and her eyes flicked open. Her need
for him was hungry and clear.

'But perhaps you're right; now is not the moment.' He
pulled back completely.

Her heart was hammering wildly against her chest. She
wanted to beg him to continue now; the ache inside her was
unbearable.

For a moment they just stared at each other. Alexi smiled
as he watched how she was battling with herself now. He
badly wanted to have sex with her, and he knew he could
just take her now…

But he wasn't going to. Because only her total acquiescence would satisfy him. He wanted her completely, not
just now but for as long as it took for him to satisfy
himself of her.

And hunger was a wonderful driving force, he told
himself vehemently. He was going to starve her now—and
later they would feast. On his terms.

He watched how her hands trembled as she started to
fasten her jeans, button up her blouse. 'We've tested the
theory,' he said smoothly. 'We still want each other, and
later we'll decide how we are going to let the chemistry
play out between us. Maybe on board the *Octavia*.'

His sheer, confident gall lashed through her. 'It's not going to happen. Alexi! I want you to keep away from me!'

He laughed at that, and the sound tormented her senses. Because, although she tried to tell herself that she was glad he had stopped, deep down she still couldn't get rid of this awful yearning. And he was obviously well aware of the fact.

'I mean it, Alexi,' she continued fiercely. 'I want more from a relationship than you will ever be able to give!'

She saw the sudden wariness in the darkness of his eyes, and it would have amused her if it hadn't hurt so much. 'And don't worry,' she assured him fervently. 'You'd be the last person I would choose for a committed relationship. I have no designs on you whatsoever. So just keep away from me! We've had our fling—it's over.'

'Well, you better tell that to your body,' he said with a wry twist of his lips. 'Tell that to your lips when they kiss me, and to your eyes when they look at me with open invitation.'

'I'm telling it to *you* now!'

She pushed past him, and with her head held high left the room. But for all her outward composure she was shaking inside. Because the truth was she still wanted him.

How could she be so weak? After all the sensible thoughts, after everything she'd been through, how could she allow herself to feel like this?

CHAPTER FIVE

IN THE moments between sleep and wakefulness the first thing Katie thought about was Alexi…and how much she missed having him in her life. It was a familiar feeling—something she had woken with most mornings since their split—but she had hoped the pain was easing recently. Now it seemed worse than ever.

She sighed and rolled over, stretching out to the cold space next to her in the warm cocoon of Egyptian cotton. She couldn't remember where she was. She could see a patch of blue sky through the window opposite, and sunlight was pouring in across the pristine-white carpets and bedding.

Then she woke up and reality came rushing back in a whoosh: the job, the long flight, the fact that she was here in Alexi's apartment and, after all her strong words and determination not to fall back under his spell, that kiss, that same familiar, deep longing…

Her heart thudded viciously against her chest as she remembered the moment—remembered the conversation—remembered that look in Alexi's eyes when she'd told him she wasn't interested in a casual affair. Wariness and unease had definitely flickered through the darkness of his gaze. Not surprising, given his commitment-phobic attitude.

She cringed. At least she had salvaged the situation and what was left of her pride by assuring him that she didn't want a serious relationship with him.

And that was true, she told herself fiercely. She didn't want to get involved with someone who would tire of her when the novelty of the passion they shared died. It would be a disaster. The sensible side of her knew that—the trouble was the passionate side of her nature was crying out for his caresses, his kisses.

This must be what it felt like to be a drug addict, she thought morosely. She knew Alexi was bad for her yet she still craved him.

She stared up at the ceiling, willing the feelings to go away. They were crazy and illogical.

OK, he was good at kissing, at making love, but she didn't really want him. It was her body playing tricks on her mind, reminding her how good things had been between them and avoiding the fact that he was everything she didn't want in a man.

She looked at her watch. It was almost eight! She'd slept for longer than she'd intended, amazing considering how wound up she'd been when she'd got into bed.

Flinging the sheets back, she reached for her short blue robe. As there was no *en suite* bathroom in her room she'd wanted to get up as early as possible so that she could shower and get back to her bedroom before Alexi woke up. Now she was on the last minute and risked bumping into him in the corridor.

She crossed to the door and listened. There was no sound in the apartment, but that didn't mean he wasn't up. Deciding to make a dash for it, she picked up her cosmetic bag, opened the door and hurried out.

Unfortunately Alexi was coming down the corridor at the same moment and she almost ran straight into him.

'Morning, Katie.' He smiled at her and immediately her stomach tied into knots.

'Morning.' She wanted to keep on walking, but he seemed to dominate the corridor so she hung back.

Unlike her he was fully dressed. She noted how stylish he looked in the pale linen suit and light-blue shirt. She also noticed the way his eyes flicked slowly over her body, making her remember those moments in his study early this morning and the way he could control her body and her mind with just a look…a touch.

'We have to leave in thirty minutes,' he told her nonchalantly.

'I'll be ready.' It was disquieting how he could look at her with intensity yet sound so coolly businesslike at the same time.

He nodded. 'I'm going across the road to the deli for something to eat and a coffee; do you want me to bring you something back?'

'No thanks.' She didn't think she could eat anything; her stomach was too busy churning with nervous apprehension.

'Sure?'

'Very sure indeed, thanks.'

His dark eyes were lingering on her face now, and she wished she'd taken the time to brush her hair. She put a self-conscious hand up to the tumble of curls and tried to push it back. 'If you will excuse me, Alexi, I'm just on my way for a shower.'

'Go right ahead.'

'I will, if you would just move out of my way.' She really didn't want to brush past him, not after their earlier encounter.

He laughed. 'Heavens, Kats, you could get a tank past me, and you're only the size of a baby doll.'

He hadn't called her Kats in a long time. It had been his pet name for her when they'd made love, and the memory of him whispering against her ear and stroking her sent a fierce wave of emotion through her.

'Don't call me that.'

'Why not? You used to like it.'

'Well, I don't now!' She glared up at him. 'This is the start of our new professional working relationship, remember? And I think we should start as we mean to go on.'

He smiled at that, and it made anger sizzle inside her—however it was an anger that started to undergo a metamorphosis as his gaze moved slowly over her scantily clad body again.

How the hell did he do this to her? she wondered in disbelief; how could he look at her like that and make her want him?

'And, just for the record, I wouldn't be walking around like this if there was an *en suite* bathroom in my room,' she assured him sharply.

'Wouldn't you?'

'No, of course not! It's most inconvenient!'

'Well, then, you better move to the room across the hallway.'

Her eyes flicked warily to the door he had indicated.

'This is a four-bed apartment, Katie,' he told her with a shake of his head. 'And you selected the only room that doesn't have *en suite* facilities.'

'Why didn't you tell me that this morning?' Her face suffused with colour.

'Well, we had other things on our mind this morning,

didn't we?' He smiled as he watched how easily she blushed. He enjoyed winding her up, enjoyed the way she threw the full fulminating heat of her gaze on him.

'You really are intolerable sometimes!' She marched past him at speed, slammed the bathroom door behind her and leaned back against it.

Damn man! He was absolutely infuriating…and infuriatingly gorgeous at the same time. The thought crept in with unwelcome force. She was sure he could get anyone he wanted into bed with just a teasing look.

Her eyes connected with her reflection in the mirror opposite. But not her, she reassured herself firmly. Not her.

She went across and turned the shower on, then took some cleansers and a body wash from her bag. She was about to slip out of her dressing gown and under the steamy hot water when she suddenly felt queasy. The feeling just hit her out of nowhere.

What on earth was wrong with her? she wondered as she clung to the side of the basin and waited for the feeling to pass. She'd had a few hours' sleep so it couldn't be tiredness. She hadn't eaten anything that would make her ill. And she couldn't be pregnant because she had done that test and it had come back negative.

A curl of apprehension stirred inside her suddenly.

But she still hadn't had her period, and it was over two months late now!

The realisation sent apprehension spinning into full-blown panic. It would be OK, she reassured herself. The test had definitely been negative, and her periods were irregular sometimes.

Even so, they were never *this* late!

She looked at herself in the mirror. Her skin was so ashen

it looked almost opaque. But she couldn't be pregnant, she told herself again. However, just to reassure herself, maybe she should buy another pregnancy-testing kit.

The boardroom was hot and stuffy, and there were so many people around the long polished table that there was hardly room to breathe.

Katie had found herself wedged between Alexi, who was presiding at the head of the meeting, and a hefty man who seemed determined to encroach into her space. One of his elbows was almost in her ribs. She tried to lean away from him, but that brought her too close to Alexi. And she would rather have been prodded to death than get too close to him.

The confines of his apartment were too much for her, never mind the space at this table! This morning had been hell. It was totally weird to be in such a close situation with a man who had once known every curve of her body intimately. How did you move on and forget that? How did you go from being lovers to sharing an apartment platonically?

And what was she going to do if she found out she was expecting his baby?

Her fingers tightened on the pen she was holding as she tried to focus on the conversation and jot down the relevant information she needed.

'So, gentlemen, if you would turn to page two you will see the chart for the projected expansion into the market,' Alexi instructed.

Katie watched as everyone dutifully turned over the pages.

She wouldn't be pregnant, she told herself calmly. She'd probably just got a stomach bug. And she did feel a lot better now.

And as for sharing the apartment it wouldn't be for

long. They'd be home tomorrow, and anyway perhaps she would just get used to being around Alexi again, and after a while all these feelings inside her would just go away of their own accord.

Their eyes met as she glanced up and immediately the theory seemed ludicrous. How could she get used to being around someone who made her whole system melt into emotional chaos?

'Katie, do you want to run through the schedules you are setting up for us?' he asked suddenly.

'Yes, of course.' She tried to inject the right amount of professionalism into her tone and squeezed back from her place to dutifully do as he had asked.

She was very conscious of his eyes following her as she stood up and went to turn on the projector so that she could make her points with the visual aid of the screen.

'As you can see, the sales are up in that sector, but we need to concentrate on our main targets.'

Alexi tried to concentrate solely on the graphs that Katie was pointing to. But she kept sidetracking him. She looked fantastic in the tight-fitting little grey suit; he could see every curve of her figure as she stretched.

'I've taken the accountants' provisional estimates and, as you see, the results are very exciting.' She flicked a switch so that the next graph came up on screen.

Not as exciting as the way she had kissed him in the early hours of the morning, or the way she had looked in that short robe... The thought crept into Alexi's mind, along with the image she had presented with her long hair tumbling around her shoulders, and her curvaceous body tantalisingly hidden by silk.

She was too damn sexy.

His eyes followed her around the table as she placed printed copies of the graphs in front of everyone. She looked very different now from the vision she had presented earlier; her hair was tied back in a severe style that showed the delicate shape of her face and her exquisite high-cheekbones. She looked sophisticated and efficient. He found it just as sexy as her earlier tousled look. He imagined kicking everyone out of the boardroom and taking her right here on the polished table. He wanted her *now*.

As if sensing his gaze, she glanced in his direction and for just a second he glimpsed distraction in her blue eyes, and the world of high finance suddenly ceased to exist.

Then she looked hastily back to the notes she was referring to.

She could pretend all she wanted, but the chemistry was still alive and kicking between them. They both knew that.

OK, it was just a sexual chemistry, but hell it was strong—stronger than anything Alexi had ever known.

He thought back to those moments in his office this morning when he'd kissed her. He had never felt so shaken up by need before! It had taken every ounce of control he possessed to pull back. And, for all Katie's pretence at coldness after that, Alexi knew if he'd touched her again he could have melted her; if he had pulled her back into his arms and kissed her he could have had her.

OK, she was suddenly professing that she wanted a serious relationship, and he certainly *didn't* want that. He didn't believe in love, he didn't want love. But he did want *her*. And the fact was she still wanted him, for all her moral high-ground. The truth of that had been there in her kiss, in her body language. It was there in the way she had just darted a look at him now.

They needed to finish what they had started and then they could both move on.

Alexi returned his attention to the paperwork on his desk.

The really bizarre thing was that she seemed to have cast some kind of weird spell over him; he just hadn't been able to move on since she'd walked out a month ago.

Every time he'd decide to take someone else to bed and forget her, a picture of her sensuous, perfectly proportioned body drifted into his mind, stopping him. He'd remember the way she could look at him with those playful, challenging blue eyes, the way her lips could curve in that secret smile that promised so much...and it had sent him crazy.

He needed her. Needed to feel her sensuous body writhing against his. It was a macho pride thing, he told himself furiously. She'd dumped him so he wanted her back—nothing more than that. Once he'd had his fill of her, these feelings would go.

Alexi frowned as he realised he was losing track of the meeting. She was still adversely affecting his work.

Later today, after business was taken care of, he would address this situation, he promised himself. And this time he wouldn't allow her to play games, he would have her exactly where he wanted her.

'So—has anyone got any questions?' Katie returned to switch off the projector.

There were one or two queries, and she answered them confidently, before suddenly diverting a question over to Alexi.

'Perhaps you'd fill everyone in on that side of things, Alexi?' She looked over at him and he noted that the blue eyes were suddenly shadowed with panic.

'Yes...of course.' He flicked to the notes he had made

earlier and answered the enquiry with half an eye on Katie as she went to the water fountain to get herself a drink. Katie would certainly have had no trouble answering that question, so why the abrupt hand-over and the look of panic?

He noted that she looked very pale suddenly, and he half rose to his feet as she swayed.

'You OK, Katie?'

'Fine.' She smiled. 'Just a bit warm in here.'

She didn't look fine. He'd thought for a moment that she was going to faint. He glanced back at the papers in front of him and decided it was time to sum things up. They'd covered the most important points and he'd had enough. Besides, she was right, it was close in here; the air conditioning didn't seem to be very efficient for some reason.

'Well, gentlemen, if there are no further questions I think we will leave it there.'

There was a murmur of dissent around the table. But Alexi had made up his mind, and he dealt with the few remaining items of business briskly. The meeting was adjourned and people rose to their feet to gather papers and leave.

Katie had never been more grateful. The room had suddenly felt like it was closing in on her, and she'd felt light-headed. She'd never fainted before in her life, but she had honestly thought she was going to black out.

She started to gather the files up and pack them away as one by one everyone left.

'The meeting seemed to go well, I think,' she murmured as Alexi came over to stand beside her.

'Yes—except for the near-fainting incident,' he answered wryly. 'What's the matter with you?'

'Nothing's the matter with me!' She flicked him an impatient glance. Did nothing escape those penetrating dark eyes?

she wondered. But inside panic was starting to take over. *What was the matter with her?* she wondered anxiously.

Just say she was pregnant?

The frantic thought thundered through her consciousness. She honestly didn't know what she would do if she was. Because if Alexi thought for one moment that she might be expecting his child he would be horrified! Just remembering how he had reacted when she had even hinted at wanting a serious relationship made that very clear. And you couldn't get anything more serious than becoming a father.

Somehow she managed to keep her voice casual. 'I think it was just too hot in here, that's all.'

'You should have had breakfast this morning.'

'You know, I could do without the lecture!' She snapped her briefcase closed. 'You look after your business and leave me to look after mine.'

'I am looking after my business. I don't want you having time off due to malnutrition!' He looked at her pointedly. 'We've got a lot to get through in the next few weeks. And I need you fit and healthy.'

'Gee, your concern really is underwhelming.'

He smiled teasingly. 'All part of the boss's job.'

How was it when he smiled at her like that she could feel her emotions squeezing? It was crazy.

It was like during the board meeting. One moment she had been totally absorbed in what she was talking about, and the next she had caught his eyes and she had just melted inside.

She looked away from him with a frown. 'While we are on the subject of work, did the accountant here send you the up-to-date figures that we asked for?' If he could be solely focussed on business then so could she, she told herself. *She had to be.* It was called self-preservation.

'Yes, he sent an email through. I'll get a printout for you.' He had to admire her, he thought wryly. She was a consummate professional; she'd obviously felt very ill, but she was still thinking about work.

'We can deal with the email after lunch,' he said dismissively. 'We'll go and have something to eat on board the *Octavia*. We may as well go down there now.'

'What time is our next meeting?' Katie asked briskly.

'Three.'

Katie glanced at her watch. She wanted to get away from him in her lunch break—she needed to get to a pharmacy and buy a pregnancy-test kit as soon as possible. 'You go on ahead and I'll catch you up later.'

'Well, you may as well come with me now,' he said. 'There's not much for you to do here.'

'I want one of the girls from the typing pool to type up my notes for me.' She stumbled a little over her words as she sought for an escape route.

'I'll get one of the secretaries down on the *Octavia* to do it for you later.'

'Yes, but I need to nip to the shops as well.' She tried to sound as casual as possible.

'If it's a dress you're looking for to wear at the party tonight, I'll get the shops on board the *Octavia* to send a selection down to my private quarters. Most of the top designer names have outlets on board. So I'm sure you'll find something you like.'

'Thanks, but I have some personal items I want to get as well.'

'Very well.' He shrugged. 'I'll let you get on with some shopping, then.'

Katie felt a flare of relief. But the feeling was short-lived as he continued briskly, 'I'll take a cab down to the docks, and my driver can drop you wherever you want and then wait for you. I'll see you back at the ship for lunch in say…' Alexi looked at his watch '…forty-five minutes.'

Katie felt her heart drop. She didn't want his driver to take her shopping—she wanted to be completely on her own. But she supposed she was being paranoid. A chauffeur wasn't going to be interested in where she went. A trip to a pharmacy was hardly breaking news, and then she supposed she could get him to drop her at a department store so that she could find a bathroom.

'OK, thanks.' She nodded. She would have agreed to anything right now to get rid of him.

They took the lift down the fifty-seven floors to street level.

It was vibrant with life outside, yellow cabs weaving amidst a river of continual traffic, pavements filled with people, whilst overhead the buildings towered into the dizzying heights of a clear blue sky, making Katie feel very small and insignificant.

The chauffeur came round and opened the rear door of the limousine.

Alexi said something to him then smiled at her. 'OK, Fred will take you wherever you want to go. Don't be late back. You need to eat lunch, and we have a business meeting at three.'

Lunch was the last thing she was bothered about.

What was she going to do if this test was positive?

CHAPTER SIX

KATIE stared at the thin blue line in disbelief. According to the test she was pregnant! How could that be—how could she have had a negative result four weeks ago and now this? Maybe she'd done the first test too early. Or maybe this test was faulty, she thought frantically. Perhaps she should buy another kit? Third time lucky and all that…

If it weren't so serious it would be funny. Because, deep down, she knew that this result was the right one.

She kept the leaflet that came with the kit and threw everything else away. Then, in a state of shock, she left the ladies' room and merged into the crowds of shoppers in the busy department store.

Saks of Fifth Avenue was a strange place to discover that she was pregnant, she thought as she walked dazedly through one department after another. But then all her surroundings were rather bizarre at the moment. Would it have been better to find out at Alexi's apartment? Or on board his ship? Maybe four weeks ago back at the shipping office before she had finished with him would have been better, but the truth was it wouldn't have made much difference. There was no best time or place because it was an absolute disaster!

How was she going to tell him? The question seared through her like an instrument of torture.

Maybe she shouldn't tell him at all. Maybe she should just check herself into a clinic somewhere and have it dealt with secretly. It was probably what he would want her to do, especially if the rumours about why his marriage had failed were true.

Alexi had never talked much to her about his marriage. She knew it had only lasted twelve months, but that was all she knew. Every time she had tried to draw him out on the subject he had clammed up or changed the conversation abruptly. It had been obvious that he didn't want to discuss it, and she hadn't wanted to press the subject, hadn't wanted him to know how much she would have liked to know the facts. Reading between the lines, she guessed Alexi had loved Andrea; he must have done to have committed to her. But they had wanted different things out of life and it had made him determined to steer clear of another full-blown relationship.

Eight years was a long time to be on his own, and she'd heard it said that if a man didn't remarry within the first couple of years after a split then it was unlikely he ever would.

In Alexi's case that was probably very true.

She noticed suddenly that she was entering the mother-and-child department. Pictures of pregnant mothers looked down at her, the women all radiantly happy in maternity wear that showed off their proud bumps.

Katie did an abrupt about-turn. She couldn't walk through there! Out of the corner of her eye she saw a cot, decorated with lace and pink frills.

It was fragile and sweet, and enough to intensify the cold churning feelings inside of her.

Could she really go through with an abortion?

And, if she didn't, how would she manage with a baby on her own? She had always sworn that she would wait until the time was right for her to have a child, because she wanted to give her baby all the things she had missed in her childhood; she wanted her to feel secure and loved. She wanted a tightly knit family unit…and that unit included a loving father.

This situation was far from her ideal dream. And how would she work and look after a child? Her job demanded long hours.

She couldn't think straight. She couldn't decide how she was going to deal with this at all!

The blare of traffic and bright sunshine hit her senses as she left the store, and it was a relief to slide into the waiting limousine and sink back into the comfortable darkened interior.

As the car sped smoothly through the traffic Katie remembered the look in Alexi's eyes only this morning when she had mentioned wanting a meaningful relationship. The word 'fatherhood' would probably freak him out completely! A baby was the biggest commitment in life.

Katie had never felt more alone in her life. And she suddenly had an overwhelming need to speak to her sister; she needed someone who would understand how she was feeling right now, and Lucy was that person.

Without even stopping to think about what time it was in France, she took out her mobile and dialled the number. But all she got was her sister's messaging service. Disappointed, Katie hung up. This wasn't the kind of predicament that could be revealed in a voicemail message.

She closed her eyes and tried to relax, tried to think logi-

cally. When was her last period—how far into the pregnancy would she be? By her reckoning, it was only two
months. However she did need to get to a doctor as soon
as possible to have things verified.

Katie didn't open her eyes again until the car had pulled
up down at the dock area and the chauffeur came round to
open the door for her.

A warm breeze washed over her, filled with the tangy
scent of the ocean, and she took deep breaths of the fresh air.

The *Octavia* was berthed a few metres away. She was
a sleek ocean-going liner with stylishly impressive lines.
Katie had worked on some of the correspondence connected with this vessel, and she knew she was one of the
most prestigious ships in Alexi's fleet, and possessed luxurious passenger accommodation and reception areas, a
shopping mall, some top celebrity-chef restaurants and
even a chapel.

If circumstances had been different she might have
enjoyed going aboard. But right now all she could think
about was escaping. How could she have lunch with Alexi
and pretend that nothing was amiss? Things had been difficult before, but they were impossible now!

She made her way down towards the gangplank where
a man in uniform was waiting.

He wanted to see her passport before allowing her on
board, and she fished it out for him.

'Welcome to the *Octavia*, Ms Connor,' he said as he
scanned it and handed it back. 'Mr Demetri has left a
message for you to go directly to his private quarters on
the top floor. Have a nice day.'

Katie continued up the gangplank and was directed
towards the lift at the end of the corridor.

She was going to have to tell Alexi. The first clear thought struck her as the lift doors opened on the top deck of the ship and she walked out. This wasn't something she could keep secret.

This was about a baby, a living entity. It wasn't just about her any more. And Alexi had a right to know.

Katie found his private suite without any difficulty; it was a few yards down from the lift. But she stood outside for a few moments, trying to gather her composure before knocking.

Her hand was poised above the door when it swung open. Alexi was on the phone taking a business call, but he waved her inside.

'This has happened before, and I can't have someone on the team making those kinds of mistakes,' he told someone forcefully. 'You will just have to get rid of him straight away. Time is of the essence.'

He sounded ruthless and determined, and Katie felt her insides tighten as she stepped into the cabin. Would he use that same forceful tone on her when she told him her news?

Get rid of it straight away. The words rebounded inside her.

And she realised with a sudden, frightening thud of reality that that wasn't what she wanted at all. She wanted this baby.

'When you've sorted the situation, phone me back.' Alexi hung up and glanced over at her.

For a moment there was silence between them.

She wanted their child, and she wanted Alexi to take her into his arms and tell her that everything would be OK.

She really was losing her grip on reality now, she thought angrily, because when she told him her news there was no way that was going to happen.

'So, how was the shopping?' Alexi took his jacket off and she was momentarily distracted by the sheer power of his body, the way his broad shoulders tapered down to the narrow hips.

'It was OK.' She tried to smile coolly.

'Did you get what you wanted?'

The question and the way his eyes flicked over her made the tension inside her escalate.

'Yes, thanks.' Somehow she managed to sound controlled.

She looked around her. Through an open doorway she could see a large double-bed. Swiftly she pulled her gaze away from that and concentrated on the lounge area where they were standing.

White, curving leather furniture followed the round contours of one side of the room, and to the other side large sliding doors gave a spectacular view out over a private deck and swimming pool. The soaring Manhattan skyline in the distance was a dramatic backdrop.

'You looked deep in thought outside the door.' The sudden observation made her look back at him with a frown.

'What do you mean?'

He waved towards a security monitor on the wall that showed the outside corridor, and she realised he'd been watching her when she'd stood outside.

'There are cameras all over the place.' He looked at her with a wry smile. 'Part of the new security measures we have introduced.'

'Very Big Brother,' she said flippantly.

'It has its uses.' He glanced at his watch. 'I ordered us lunch, by the way. I took a wild guess at what you would want.'

'Did you? How very cavalier of you.'

Alexi glanced over and his eyes held a sudden gleam of amusement. 'The house salad…and a side order of fries. Sound about right?'

It was what she had always ordered when they were having a working lunch. And she had always joked that she shouldn't eat the fries, but that they were her one sin for the afternoon. And Alexi would smile and say *we'll see about that!*

She didn't want to remember things like that. She didn't want to remember the ease and the passion between them—because it hadn't been real, she reminded herself fiercely. And it didn't help with this situation now.

She shrugged. 'To be honest, I'm not really that hungry.'

He frowned. 'Are you still feeling ill?'

'No, I'm not ill.' She looked away from him. 'But you're right, I should eat something. Thanks.'

Before he could comment further there was a knock on the door.

It was the staff with their lunch. Katie was very glad of the interruption. She watched as a table was put out on a shady part of the deck and laid with a pristine-white cloth and silverware. The scene looked inviting and intimate—nothing like a working lunch.

This was probably the best time to tell him. The knowledge thumped through her as they were left alone again.

Alex held the door open for her to precede him out to the table, and she practised the words in her head: *Alexi, I think I'm pregnant. But don't worry, I'll deal with it myself.*

The pronouncement filtered through her like ice water.

Being a single mother was going to be hard…really hard. Just say she made all the same mistakes her mother had made? Just say she went from one bad relationship to another and her baby never knew security, never knew a

loving father. She stopped the panic-stricken thoughts
before they could start to get a grip.

This wasn't helping. Lots of women brought up children
alone and they made a brilliant job of it. She would be one
of *those* women—she was nothing like her mother.

'Glass of wine?' Alexi asked.

'I won't, thanks. We have a lot of work to get through
this afternoon,' she said firmly.

'Always so sensible,' he murmured.

She didn't feel particularly sensible, she felt like she was
drowning in a sea of reckless uncertainty. But she forced
herself just to smile. 'That's one of the reasons you like
having me around, isn't it? Or so you used to tell me.'

'One of the reasons…yes.' His dark eyes seemed to burn
into her. 'The other reason is that you blend sexy with sensible
so well. It's a unique combination, very hard to resist.'

The husky words jarred inside her.

'Don't mock me, Alexi.'

He frowned, something in her tone touching him. She
looked very young suddenly, and very vulnerable. 'Katie,
I wasn't mocking you,' he said quietly.

For a few short moments the air between them seemed
to overflow with emotions that Katie couldn't fathom. All
she knew was that she wanted to go into his arms so badly
that it hurt.

But there was no going back, she reminded herself
firmly, especially now.

If she allowed him to touch her, allowed him to take her
to bed, it would just be sex. Alexi had nothing to offer her
in the way of commitment. There would always be the next
conquest waiting for him.

Their eyes clashed across the table.

And maybe now wasn't the right time to tell him about the baby. She didn't think she was strong enough; her emotions were all over the place, and she needed to be really sure about what she wanted before she could discuss it with him.

She sought for a means of escape and found it in work. 'How do you think my ideas went down at the meeting today?' she asked, taking off her jacket, trying to act as if she didn't notice the mood between them.

Alexi knew that she was deliberately hiding behind work. His eyes flicked down over her, noticing how her white shirt was unbuttoned just enough to show the lacy curve of her bra. He felt the heat of desire escalate inside him, and he wondered if he should allow her to hide from the real agenda between them quite so easily.

Then he looked back into her eyes and saw the glimmer of answering need, mixed with a sudden helplessness. It was an expression he'd never seen in her eyes before.

After a slight hesitancy he allowed her to escape, allowed the conversation to continue. 'There were a few people who seemed unsure about whether or not you could achieve the results in such a short time-frame,' he said nonchalantly. 'But all in all I think your ideas were well received.'

What was really going through her mind? Alexi wondered as he poured them both a glass of water from the jug on the table. He knew she still desired him…and he had the sudden very strong feeling that this was about more than her just wanting to move on. 'I also think you are going to have to spend some more money on advertising,' he continued. 'Your figures aren't stacking up in that particular area.'

'Yes they are!' Katie frowned. 'I've researched thoroughly, and it is a balanced plan of action between TV and the national papers. It will be enough for an initial launch.'

'Ah, but we don't want it to be just enough, we want it to be lavish and extravagant.'

Alexi sat back and watched as she defended her schedule. Her eyes were vivid with enthusiasm now.

She put the water down and reached for her briefcase. 'We can run through the figures again, if you want?' She took out the notes she had made earlier and placed them on the table beside her plate.

It was as if she was building a barricade, Alexi thought wryly. And he wasn't going to allow her to go that far! It was time to move to the truth…reel her in.

'I don't think so.' He met her eyes steadily. 'I think we have other things to talk about over lunch. Time enough for that conversation later.'

Immediately the wary light was back in her eyes. 'Alexi, if this is about what happened between us earlier today then I really don't think there is anything else to say.'

'Don't you?' He fixed her with that steady look that seemed to burn into her consciousness.

And she could feel herself colouring up as the enormity of the lie hit her. There *was* something else to say…something he needed to know.

Her mobile phone started to ring and she took it out of her bag with a decidedly shaky hand and looked at the screen. It was her sister.

'Excuse me…' She started to push her chair back from the table. 'I'm going to have to take this call.'

'No, you are not.' Alexi reached out and calmly took it off her and severed the connection.

'How dare you do that?' She got to her feet and glared at him, furious with him.

'You can phone whoever it is back later.' Alexi put the

phone down on the table and sat back with a frown. Something was wrong, and he couldn't put a finger on what it was. Maybe it was nothing. Maybe it was just that he wasn't used to being given the runaround like this. He didn't like it; he felt edgy and uneasy.

'Sit down,' he ordered.

For a moment she didn't comply, but then he looked at her with those ruthlessly intense eyes and she did as she was told, her heart thumping unmercifully hard against her chest.

'We need to clear the air, Katie.'

'I don't think we can.' She said the words with a sudden raw honesty. 'I think I need to give my notice in!' The words spilled out before she could think about them, before she could stop them. OK, it wasn't something she had planned to do: she would be pregnant without a job! But she would get something else, she told herself. *Anything else.* She needed to get away.

That sudden fact burned with real force. She couldn't stay—not now that she was expecting his child. It would be a disaster—it would be impossible!

Alexi's eyes narrowed on her. 'I think that's called running away, Katie.'

'I think it's called being realistic.' She raised her chin and glared at him.

'You've signed a four-month contract with the company. That is being realistic.' He frowned. 'This isn't like you, Katie,' he remarked abruptly. 'You and I are very similar, we both put work first. And you've only just started on this project! Now you want to run away because of the chemistry between us?'

He sounded angry and his eyes seemed to burn into hers.

She needed to tell him about the baby…she needed to say it now!

A breeze fluttered the papers that Katie had left next to her and suddenly they flurried everywhere, over the table and down over the deck, making them both spring up to catch them.

Their hands met as they both reached for the last page before it blew into the pool, and Katie let go as if she had been burnt. Slowly they both stood up. He was very close to her, and she felt an ache of need to just go into his arms.

'So what is this about, Katie?' he asked her softly. 'Surely it's not just about the fact that you kissed me this morning? That there is still a sexual attraction between us?'

Her cheeks flared with colour. She noticed he'd said *she'd* kissed *him*, not the other way around. And he was right; she had been the one to reach for him. The fact stung through her with humiliating clarity.

Her mobile was ringing again. She wrenched away from him angrily and went to pick it up.

'Hi, Lucy…can I phone you back a bit later? I can't talk right now.' As she was speaking she watched Alexi open the front flap of her briefcase to put the papers away.

Then she stiffened as she saw him glance at the leaflet she had placed in there earlier.

He looked at it, and then looked at it again, then he pulled it out of the bag.

'Why is there a leaflet about pregnancy in amongst your work papers?' he asked coolly.

He transferred his gaze over towards her as she put the phone down. 'Katie, what is this about?'

CHAPTER SEVEN

SHOCK ricocheted through Alexi as he watched the blood drain from her face, and suddenly things started to fall into place.

'I asked you a question, Katie.' He walked over and placed the leaflet down in front of her, and their eyes met. 'What is this?'

The coolness of his voice was not in keeping with the sudden flame in his eyes.

'It's the real reason I can't stay...' she whispered the words uncomfortably. 'I'm pregnant, Alexi.'

It was hard to tell what was running through Alexi's mind. His dark eyes were now inscrutable. She could see a pulse beating at the side of his jaw. 'Is the baby mine?' he demanded at last.

'Of course it's yours!' She took a step back from him, her distress escalating at the question.

'So how long have you been keeping this from me?'

'I haven't been keeping it from you! I've just told you now!'

'Because you had to!'

She'd known of course that he would be angry, but the

full extent of the rage she glimpsed in his eyes at that moment was truly scary.

'That's not true.' She brushed her hands tiredly over her face. 'I was working up to it, I just didn't know how to tell you.'

He didn't say anything to that.

'To be honest with you, Alexi, I haven't come to terms with the fact myself yet,' she continued heatedly.

The expression in his eyes didn't change.

'I was trying to think things through properly, allow my mind to clear so that I would know what I wanted to do before we talked.'

'And how long was that going to take?'

She had never heard so much hostility in his tone.

'Would it have been before you got rid of the baby, or after?'

'How dare you say something like that to me?' Anger rose like bile in her throat.

'How dare you try to hide this from me?' He came closer, and she could see condemnation etched in his expression like stone. 'Is this the reason you gave in your notice the first time around?'

'No! I didn't know I was pregnant back then!' She was horrified by the accusation. 'I admit I did a test before we split up, but it came back negative. It scared the hell out of me, Alexi, it made me realise that our casual affair was dangerous territory!'

He stepped back from her.

'Then I started to feel sick this morning, and I nearly passed out at the meeting, and suddenly I started to wonder if the test I did back then was accurate.'

She watched as he raked a hand through the darkness

of his hair. 'So in a panic I ran out and bought another one today. I couldn't believe it when it came back with a positive result! I…I didn't know what to say, what to do…'

He shook his head. 'So the first thing you do is try to quit your job—try and walk away without even telling me.' His voice was dry.

'For heaven's sake, Alexi, give me a break! My emotions are all over the place.' Her voice cracked. 'I admit I haven't been thinking straight. But I'm probably still in shock!'

He nodded as if he accepted that, but the silence between them was loaded with tension.

'So this morning, when you talked about wanting a more serious relationship, were you thinking about this situation?' He asked the question bluntly.

'No, I wasn't even contemplating this situation!' Her head jerked up and for a second her eyes blazed into his. 'And you don't need to worry, Alexi. You're not involved in this at all. This is my baby. And if I do decide to go ahead with the pregnancy I won't want anything from you,' she continued emphatically. 'You won't be committed to anything, time or money.'

Something in Alexi's eyes hardened now. 'You can think again about that, Katie,' he said quietly. 'I'm involved in this whether you like it or not!'

'You can't force me into making a decision I don't want! I will do what's right for me at the end of the day—'

'But this isn't just about you any more!' He cut across her angrily.

'Do you think I don't know that?' She flared. 'The responsibility for this feels huge, it's already crushing me.'

'Which is why we will have to share it.' His tone was resolved.

'We don't have to do anything of the kind!'

'Don't fight me on this, Katie, because you will lose.' The strength of his tone made her quake inside.

He walked away from her and looked out across the water towards the distant skyline of Manhattan. And for a long moment neither spoke.

'You can't make me have a termination if I don't want one!' Her voice trembled.

'I haven't mentioned the word "termination".' He looked around at her calmly.

'*Yet.*' She glared at him. 'But I know what you are thinking. You're thinking that if you pay for a private clinic and an abortion that that will absolve you—that will be your share of the responsibility, or at least as much of a share as you would *want*.' Her words were tinged with bitter emphasis. 'You just want the problem to go away.'

'You don't know the first thing about what I'm thinking right now!' he told her heavily.

'I know *you*! I know that you are commitment-phobic— and that you are the last person in the world who would want to become a dad!'

'I admit since my marriage ended I've steered clear of serious relationships.' He turned and gave her his full attention again. 'But that doesn't give you the right to judge me over this!'

She looked at him through narrowed eyes. 'You didn't want children when you were married, never mind now! I've heard the rumours.'

He became very still. 'Have you, indeed?'

'Yes! You didn't want children and your ex-wife did.' Katie waded in; she was past caring what he thought now. 'So don't stand there pretending to be something you are not. Don't think you can pull the wool over my eyes, and then gently suggest an expensive little clinic when the moment's right!'

'You don't know what the hell you are talking about, Katie.' Alexi's voice was low, but filled with such a quiet fury that it made her shiver.

'I'm sorry.' She was momentarily back-footed. 'I probably shouldn't have said that.'

'No you shouldn't!'

'You've never talked about your marriage with me, so—'

'So you went with the gossip-mongers' version of events.' He looked at her scathingly. 'Just for the record, Katie, I loved my wife—and I would have done anything for her. But you're right—once my marriage broke up I decided it was an institution best avoided. I decided not to invest again in any real relationships. Casual affairs were all I wanted, and I certainly had no plans to start a family.'

Katie tried to ignore how that acknowledgement made her feel, tried to quash down the pain that simmered beneath the surface. She knew she didn't mean anything to him. It was old news, she told herself staunchly.

She tipped her chin up proudly. 'So you don't need to concern yourself with this pregnancy now. Because I'm not asking you to invest in anything, Alexi—emotionally or otherwise. I saw the way you looked at me this morning when I even mentioned wanting a meaningful relationship! And don't worry,' she continued hurriedly, 'I really wasn't hinting at anything, I really didn't know I was pregnant at that moment. And I meant it when I said I didn't think we would be right together. What we had was just a fling, it wasn't supposed to end like this!'

'No, it wasn't,' he agreed with her quietly. 'We were careful, we took precautions. But accidents happen.'

Something inside Katie twisted.

His eyes held with hers. 'It's how we deal with this from here on in that matters now.'

She nodded and tried to swallow down a lump in her throat.

Alexi noticed how tired she looked suddenly, her eyes over-bright in the pallor of her face. And he remembered how she had nearly passed out this morning. 'You need to sit down,' he said abruptly.

The sudden concern in his voice was not welcome. And it helped her to pull herself together. She didn't want his kindness; she would rather have dealt with his anger, at least it was fervently meant. 'I'm fine, Alexi.' She met his gaze defiantly. 'I'm not an invalid, and I don't need you to start treating me like one.'

He smiled at that. 'That was the furthest thing from my mind, believe me. But you should sit down, and you should eat something.' He moved back to the table. 'You haven't eaten all day.'

The last thing she felt like doing was eating—especially seated opposite him. Her throat felt so tightly closed with emotion that she felt the food might choke her.

But she did as he suggested and reached for a glass of water.

For a few moments there was silence between them.

'How far do you think the pregnancy has progressed?' He asked the question almost casually as he settled back into his chair.

'Two months—I think.' She shrugged and couldn't meet his gaze now. 'I'll get everything confirmed by a doctor.'

'I'll make an appointment for you to see Richard Hall this afternoon.'

She looked over at him questioningly.

'He's the ship's doctor,' Alexi enlightened her.

'How convenient.'

'Yes,' he agreed with her briskly. 'And we'll take it from there.'

'You suddenly sound like you are organising a business campaign,' she muttered angrily.

'We have to be practical, Katie.'

Their eyes met, and Katie wanted to tell him that she would have given anything to put practicality to one side right now. And that she longed just to be held in his arms. But she forced herself to just agree, because he was right, and because anything else would be foolish in the extreme. 'Yes, of course.'

'You may as well take the rest of the afternoon off,' he continued as he glanced at his watch.

'I'd rather keep busy, and we have a meeting at three.'

'We've dealt with the important stuff this morning. You can miss the next meeting.'

Alexi's mobile started to ring and he snapped it up impatiently. 'I'll be there in a minute,' he told whoever was at the end of the line before closing the connection again. 'I have to go, Katie. I'll ask the doctor to ring you so you can make that appointment and we'll discuss things later.'

Katie shrugged. There was no point arguing with Alexi when he used that tone.

Richard Hall was a pleasant man in his late forties. He'd given Katie a thorough examination and then declared that she was in perfect health and just over two months pregnant.

'Congratulations,' he'd told her jovially. 'You are going to have an early and very special Christmas present. I'd say the baby is due about the twentieth of December.'

She was lying back on the bed in the cabin now, trying to get her head around everything. Trying to visualise her small flat at Christmas—the usual decorations, the cards, the Christmas tree, the *baby's cot*! It seemed unreal.

But it was real, she told herself powerfully. And she wanted this baby with all her heart. That certainty was growing stronger and stronger inside her. No matter what Alexi said to her, he wasn't going to make her change her mind about that.

All right, it would be difficult to manage alone, and realistically she knew she would struggle financially. It would probably help her to keep her job here with Alexi—it was only a four-month contract, but it would enable her to save enough for a decent nest-egg. After that she could look around for part-time work.

The trouble was that she didn't think she was emotionally strong enough to stay around Alexi, and her first instinct of just quitting and walking away was still spinning around temptingly. After all, what kind of an atmosphere would there be if she stayed? If Alexi wanted her to get rid of the baby and she refused it could be grim. On the other hand she couldn't bear his reluctant conformity either...or his charity.

She closed her eyes as she remembered his reaction to her news. His anger had been even more intense than she had expected, and then it was as if he had undergone an almost steely resignation.

The memory made her curl up into a tight ball.

Snippets of his conversation kept playing painfully through her mind.

*Just for the record, Katie, I loved my wife—and I would
have done anything for her... I decided not to invest again
in any real relationships. Casual affairs were all I wanted,
and I certainly had no plans to start a family.*

She put her hand protectively on her stomach. 'We'll
manage without him,' she whispered fiercely. 'We don't
need him.'

The sound of the main cabin-door opening made her sit
up. Hurriedly she got to her feet and checked her appearance in the mirror over the dressing table.

She looked pale, and her hair was loose and tousled around
her shoulders. But there wasn't much she could do about her
appearance, as she'd left her bag out in the lounge area of the
cabin. She combed her fingers through her hair and rubbed
her lips together to get some colour back into them.

'Katie?' There was a knock on the bedroom door. Before
she could gather herself to answer, Alexi opened the door.

His eyes moved over her, assessing her with almost
ruthless intensity. 'How are you feeling?'

'Fine.' She wanted to say something flippant like, *and
still pregnant*, but she held her tongue. There was a ton of
emotion churning inside her. He looked so casually handsome, jacket slung over his shoulder, his white shirt unbuttoned at the neck.

'How did the meeting go?' She asked the question more
for something to say than any real interest.

'The accountants were impressed with your plans.' He
came into the room and tossed the jacket down onto the
chair in the corner. 'You'll be pleased to know they backed
your ideas one-hundred percent.'

'Good.'

He transferred his attention over to her completely now.

This was all a little too intimate for Katie's peace of mind. To the outsider it would have looked as if they were a couple, perfectly at ease together in the bedroom. But they were not. She was anything but at ease.

'I saw the doctor,' she told him awkwardly.

'Yes, he told me, you're just over two months pregnant.'

Her eyes widened slightly. 'He told you?'

Alexi frowned. 'Is there a problem with that?'

'Yes, there's a problem!' She hadn't planned on saying that, it just came out. 'This is my baby, and I would like my confidentiality respected!'

'It is respected. And, as I told Richard when I made you the appointment today, it's my baby, too.'

'Don't do this, Alexi!' Her voice trembled.

'Do what?' For a moment his eyes flicked over her, taking in the tumble of curls around her shoulders. She looked pale and fragile but utterly beautiful.

'Try to take me over.' She glared at him.

'Take you over...' He repeated the words and for a moment looked amused.

'I know you, Alexi,' she reminded him. 'I know what a shrewd operator you are. You're treating this situation as if it is some business plan that you are in charge of. Well, it's not! I'm in charge of this.'

The amusement suddenly died in his eyes. 'I told you earlier, Katie, I won't be sidelined—this is my child. I'm involved whether you like it or not...and I want this baby.'

'You *want* the baby?' She stared at him in surprise.

'Yes.'

She continued just to look up at him with startled suspicion. 'You *really* want the baby?'

'*Yes*. I just said so.'

'Mr Commitment-Phobic? Mr "I only want casual relationships" wants to take on the biggest responsibility there is in life…a baby?'

'Don't be facetious, Katie, it doesn't suit you.'

'Well, come on, Alexi, you've got to admit it is a bit of a leap for you, isn't it?'

He shrugged. 'But every journey in life has to start with a single step, doesn't it?' He looked into her eyes. 'We've taken that step—there's no going back.'

She felt a warm feeling of relief start to wind its way through her body. She'd hardly dared hope that he would say something like that to her, and that this was going to be OK.

'I want this baby, too.' She whispered the words, her voice unsteady as emotion shivered through her. 'So much it hurts.'

'So we are in agreement.' He said the words gently, and for a moment his eyes held with hers. 'I'm glad, Katie. It simplifies everything. A baby needs the security of a mother and a father.'

She could drown in his eyes, she thought hazily. Her gaze moved to the gleam of satisfaction on his sensual lips.

'So we'll get married,' he told her softly.

'What did you just say?' For a moment she thought she had misheard him.

'We'll get married,' he told her again, his tone supremely confident. 'As soon as I can arrange it.'

For a few startled moments her mind played with the proposal. 'But we don't love each other,' she whispered.

'Does that really matter?' He held her gaze seriously. 'That emotion only complicates things anyway.'

She was jolted back to reality with an abruptness that made her blink. 'Of course it matters!'

'Katie, giving our child a secure upbringing is what

matters! Think about it, you can't possibly manage on your own. For a start you live in a tiny first-floor apartment—totally unsuitable.'

'I'll manage perfectly well!' She glared at him.

He shook his head. 'Anyway, you don't have to. You are expecting my heir; obviously I'm going to look after you.'

'By taking over my life.' Something hardened inside Katie.

'By doing the right thing.'

'Well, I don't want you to do the right thing!' For some strange reason she wanted to cry. 'And if that is your idea of a proposal you can keep it.'

He fixed her with a piercing look. 'It's my idea of a solution,' he said calmly.

'Well, I don't like it.'

'So what do you suggest, then?' He looked at her with a raised eyebrow. 'Do you think it would be better if I wait until the child is born and then take you forcibly to court because I want custody?'

'You wouldn't do that!' Her breath seemed to freeze in her throat.

'Katie, I'll do whatever it takes,' he told her powerfully. 'And, believe me, you don't want to be on the wrong side of me. Because I have the money and resources to go all the way, and I will win.'

'A judge wouldn't give you custody!' Her voice wasn't quite steady now. 'No right-minded person would take a baby from its mother!'

'Let's see…take a baby from a one-parent family and transport it into the loving network of one of the richest, most powerful dynasties in Europe?'

She swallowed hard. The feeling of initial relief that he wanted his child had now turned to a feeling of complete fear. 'I can't believe you are saying these things! That you could even contemplate for a moment forcibly removing a child from its mother—it's barbaric!'

'I wasn't contemplating it,' he told her calmly. 'I'm hoping you will see sense and it won't come to that.'

See sense! The words sizzled through her. He was offering her marriage like he was offering a deal in the boardroom.

'You may have more money than me, but that doesn't make up for love, Alexi! A judge would look at both sides of the equation.'

'You think my child won't be loved?' He looked at her with a quizzical expression. 'You must think very little of me if you believe that. OK, you and I are not *in love*, but that doesn't mean I'm incapable of loving! And I want the best for my child, and that includes a mother—a loving family-unit.'

The words made her emotions swirl in confusion.

'You are a part of that, Katie...I want you in my life.'

But he didn't really want her—not in the way a man usually meant when he suggested marriage. 'You want me as some kind of convenient baby-minder, you mean!' she told him bitterly.

'No, I want you as my wife...in my bed.' He came closer and reached out a hand to stroke it lightly down over the side of her face. It was a gentle, almost tender caress and it made her emotions ache with the need to turn towards him, lift her face for his kiss.

'A marriage without love would never work.' She tried to keep focussed on reality.

For a moment anger swirled inside Alexi. He couldn't believe that she was trying to turn him down! He hadn't been able to think about anything else this afternoon—and the more he thought about it, the more sense this made. In fact, he couldn't believe the ache inside him—the passionate intensity with which he now knew he wanted her. Because of the child, of course—not because of the desire she stirred in him. He could click his fingers and have a harem of women if he wanted. He didn't need her. But, by God, he was going to have her!

'We may not be head over heels in love, but we are compatible, Katie,' he told her, his tone forceful. 'Especially in the bedroom.'

For a moment his eyes rested on her lips, and she felt herself tremble inside as she remembered what had happened between them only this morning. He was right—she had never wanted anyone the way she wanted him. Whatever emotion lay between them, it was powerfully compelling.

'I only have to touch you and you want me,' he murmured.

She shook her head, trying to fight against the whispering voices inside that were telling her he was right. 'You are the most arrogant man I have ever met!' she told him fiercely instead.

'You said that this morning, before you kissed me.' He smiled and watched how her skin flared with uncomfortable heat.

'I am a truthful man, Katie.' He stroked his hand down over her face, tipping her chin upwards so that she was forced to look at him. He watched the shadows flicking through the beauty of her blue eyes, watched as her lips parted involuntarily. 'I can feel the heat of your desire when I touch you. I can taste it when I kiss you…'

He came closer and, before she could break away, his lips captured hers, his hand holding her still and compliant. She felt a surge of longing so deep that it shook her to the core.

Intuitively she opened her mouth for him and kissed him back. She moved a little closer, her heart thundering against her ribs so heavily, so loudly, it drowned out the warning voices inside her head. All she knew was that she wanted him so much, wanted him to touch her intimately, make love to her…take away this craving need for him.

He was the one to break the spell and pull away. 'You see?' He smiled down at her.

His arrogant confidence seared through her. She didn't know who she was more furious with, him, or herself for instantly responding with such heat. 'I don't see anything.' She tried to shrug the feelings away.

'You need more proof?' he asked lazily. 'Shall we try it again?'

'No! Stop it, Alexi!' Her voice broke on a small cry of panic, and he laughed.

'You see, it will work between us! So why risk everything by going it alone?'

His flippant attitude hurt. 'It wouldn't be a risk. Not if you were a reasonable person!'

'I am being reasonable, Katie. I'm offering you marriage. I don't want our child torn apart by a court, by feuding parents! I want him to have the same secure upbringing that I enjoyed as a child in Greece.'

'You'd take him out of the country?' She looked at him in horror.

'Of course. His heritage is Greek, and I have a large family-network. He would be secure within that network.'

'And just say the baby is a girl?' she snapped. 'You might not be so interested then.'

'The sex of the child is unimportant to me! You think a girl doesn't need a father?'

The question splintered through her. She knew a girl needed a father; she knew a child needed a secure family no matter what their gender. She knew from personal experience how important it was to feel part of a family, to feel secure and safe.

'So what is it to be, Katie? Are you going to accede to my wishes and put our child first, or is this going to develop into a battle for custody?' he asked.

She shrugged, but her eyes flashed fire at him as she tried to pretend that he wasn't scaring her, and that she was in control of this. 'I'll think about it.'

He looked at her with a flicker of admiration. 'We'll make a good team,' he reflected.

'I only said I'd think about it!' she reminded him angrily.

He smiled. 'You can give me your answer tonight at the party.'

'No, Alexi, I won't be rushed!'

'And I won't be kept waiting. Once I have made up my mind about something, I am not a patient man.'

There was a knock on the outer cabin-door.

'That's probably the boutique with the selection of cocktail dresses I told them to bring down for you.' Alexi glanced at his watch. 'I'll let them in on my way out. And I'll see you up on deck later for your answer, say about six-thirty, before the party gets into full swing.'

She watched helplessly as he walked away. She had once heard it said that Alexander Demetri always got what he wanted—but she'd thought that the reference was mostly concerned with his business life. She'd seen his steely determination on many occasions in boardroom meetings, had often felt sorry for anyone who stood in the way of his objectives. However she had never glimpsed his ruthless determination on a personal basis. Not, that was, until today. And it was a formidable experience.

If he took her to court, he would probably win!

CHAPTER EIGHT

ALEXI stood by the ship's rail, looking out to sea. The sun was setting in a golden haze, sending light spinning out across the horizon, turning the water to gold.

If someone had told him this morning that by the time the sun went down he would have made a proposal of marriage, he would have laughed scornfully. Yet here he was, awaiting Katie's answer, and not just with cool indifference—this felt more like he was imploding with impatient need.

He had always trusted his instincts. It was his gut instinct that had helped him turn the family shipping business into a global phenomenon, it was his instinct that had guided him every step of the way until he controlled a worldwide business-empire.

His one mistake had been his marriage.

But he'd told himself that everyone was allowed to make one mistake, and he had promised himself that it would never happen again. He would never take those vows again; he would never love a woman again.

And he had meant it.

But life had a way of laughing mockingly at your promises, and of opening up alternative paths—paths that forced you into making difficult choices.

OK, this wasn't a love match. He would never feel the way he'd felt about Andrea again; that kind of love only led to pain.

But Katie was having his baby!

And he desired her...fiercely desired her. The need to take her back to bed had been eating away at him for weeks. Even when she had told him this morning that she wanted a relationship that was more solid, more serious, he hadn't been able to let go of the feelings he had for her. The sexual chemistry had simply been too strong.

When he had discovered she was pregnant a minefield of fierce emotions had opened up inside him. Part of him had been transported back to the past, back to Andrea. He'd hardly been able to look at Katie without seeing Andrea...without remembering that day when he had discovered the truth.

But that was the past, he told himself. Katie and their baby was the future.

And when Katie had looked up at him and had told him she wanted their child he had known beyond a doubt that marriage was the right way forward.

At thirty-five he was not getting any younger. And his business empire did need an heir. His father had been hammering on about that for long enough!

The warmth of the evening air reminded him of Greece, and his thoughts drifted towards home. He owned a sprawling mansion on ten acres of ocean front. The views out across the sea were spectacular. There was an orchard and a swimming pool.

He'd inherited it from his grandparents, who had hoped that one day he would live there with his wife and children. But it hadn't been to Andrea's tastes, she'd preferred to live in the city, so it had lain closed up for all these years. Alexi rarely went there. It wasn't a practical proposition to live there as a bachelor, it was too big, and his apartments in Athens, London and New York were more convenient.

But now everything had changed. Suddenly the place seemed very practical. He found himself wondering what the garden would look like now as spring turned to summer; he imagined the blossom of the fruit trees, the rich fragrance of the heavily ripened figs so evocative of the Greek summers. There was nowhere quite as beautiful as Greece, he thought nostalgically. His childhood had been idyllic and it was what he wanted for his own son or daughter.

Suddenly he longed to be back there.

Tomorrow. Tomorrow he would leave with Katie for Athens. But before that they would be married in the chapel here on board the *Octavia*.

Now that he had made up his mind he didn't see the point in waiting around. He'd already spoken to lawyers and put the wheels in motion. Legally they needed twenty-four hours—he'd spoken to a judge, he'd spoken to the captain here on board…everything was arranged. All he needed was Katie's compliance, and he would get that.

He turned away from the view. The band was tuning up, ready for the evening ahead. Trestle tables loaded with food were set alongside tables and chairs for about a hundred people, and a dance area had been set up around the pool.

He was throwing this party as a thank-you to his staff for working so hard to get the refit of the *Octavia* finished on schedule. A few people had already arrived, the men in dark tuxedos, the women in evening dresses. He glanced at his watch and wondered where Katie was. He hadn't managed to get down to the suite again. Business had swallowed the rest of the afternoon, to the extent where it had been quicker to shower and change back at his apartment whilst he'd been in town.

'Alexi, how nice to see you.' He turned as a business associate came over to shake his hand and introduce him to his wife, an elegant woman in her thirties.

He tried to concentrate on what they were saying, but at the back of his mind all he could think about was Katie. He wanted her answer. Where the hell was she? he wondered impatiently. It was almost seven now!

He was about to excuse himself and go looking for her, when a door further along the deck opened and Katie stepped out.

Captivated, Alexi watched as she walked gracefully across to the ship's rail to look out at the view. She looked sensational; the strapless black cocktail-dress was sculpted to her curves, and showed off her flawless figure and long legs to perfection. Her dark hair was loose and tumbled in spiral curls the colour of rich mahogany around her creamy bare shoulders.

As if sensing his gaze, she looked around, and as their eyes connected Alexi felt a fierce thrust of desire.

'Alexi, do you agree?' He was vaguely aware that the woman beside him was waiting for an answer to some question.

He frowned impatiently and dragged his eyes away from Katie for a second. 'Clare, my apologies,' he murmured smoothly. 'I've just seen someone I need to talk to.'

'Yes, but do you agree?' The woman had her hand on Alexi's sleeve, as if loathe to let him escape.

He didn't have a damn clue what she was talking about. 'Claire…' He turned the full force of his smile on the woman.

'We'll have to take up this conversation a little later.' With a nod towards the woman's husband, he extricated himself and strode purposefully away towards his quarry.

Katie looked back across the water towards Manhattan and tried to feign nonchalance, but she was acutely aware that Alexi was walking towards her. The way he had just looked at her had sent scalding-hot waves of panic and desire shooting through every nerve ending in her body.

He was going to want an answer to his proposal, and she didn't know what that answer was. She had spent the last few hours trying to recover her equilibrium, trying to tell herself that she didn't need to rush this decision, that he would just have to wait. But he didn't look like a man who was prepared to wait.

There was something so determined about his every step, his every look, that she could feel those calm, rational thoughts starting to dissolve.

'Good evening, Katie; you're late!' Alexi's tone was cool. Yet his eyes seemed to burn into hers as she looked up at him.

'Am I?' She shrugged. 'I was reading a few notes from the meeting this morning, I must have lost track of time.' It was a blatant lie; she had stared at her notes and tried to read them, but all she had been able to think about was Alexi's proposal.

'Were you, indeed?' Alexi felt a flicker of impatience. He had always liked the fact that she was as obsessed about work as he was—it had suited him. But it didn't suit him now.

He noticed she wore little make-up, just a sprinkling of gold along the dark line of her lashes, and a hint of red gloss on her lips. She looked young and freshly innocent.

'Well, I guess you were worth waiting for,' he added huskily. 'You look lovely.'

'Thank you.' She couldn't quite control her blush, and he smiled.

He found the contrasts of her character fascinating—one moment she was the strong, confident businesswoman, and the next she was his innocent mistress again, the woman who had pleased him so well in the bedroom, who had responded to him with such sweet hesitancy, as if almost afraid by the turbulence of their passion.

How had he allowed her to slip away from him these last few weeks? He was angry with himself for letting that happen. One thing was sure—it wouldn't happen again! 'So, have you thought about my offer, Katie?'

The abruptness of the question was intensely disquieting. 'Are we talking about work now or your marriage proposal?' she grated sarcastically.

'You know very well what I'm talking about.'

'Yes, unfortunately I do. But what I can't understand is how can you treat the subject of marriage as if it were a mere business proposition.' She asked the question with raw emphasis.

'Actually, like it or not, marriage *is* a business proposition,' he told her bluntly. 'It *is* a legal partnership.'

'You sound like a lawyer,' she murmured. 'But then, you did train and qualify as a lawyer, didn't you?' she reflected suddenly. 'I remember you telling me that now.'

'What has that got to do with anything?' he demanded with irritation.

'A great deal, believe me.' She flicked her chin up proudly. 'Because I don't want to be trapped in a cold, businesslike marriage, Alexi!'

He laughed at that. 'Katie, honey, who are you kidding? The heat between us is like a furnace.'

As his eyes drifted down over her, the truth of that remark was all too obvious; she felt herself tremble inside as she recalled just how deeply he could satisfy her.

How did you fight your feelings for someone who could look at you and turn you into a quivering mass of longing? she wondered hazily.

Well, she was damned if she was going to be a pushover, she told herself firmly. She had her pride, and marriage to a man who didn't love her would take some swallowing. She wasn't sure she could go through with it...even for the sake of her child.

But what were the alternatives? Facing Alexi in a courtroom for a custody battle? The very thought made her nerves twist anxiously. Not only could he buy and sell her for breakfast, he knew the law inside out—he would annihilate her!

'Alexi, did you mean it when you said you would fight me for custody?' She flicked him an uncertain look.

'I never say anything I don't mean,' he answered her steadily. 'But I don't want to do that. I don't want to hurt you.'

'Then don't!' Her voice broke slightly.

'Then don't make me!' he countered her plea, his eyes unyielding. 'This is about more than just you, Katie,' he reminded her. 'This is about a child—the heir to the Demetri fortune, no less!'

'That's all that matters to you, isn't it? That you have "control" of your precious son and heir.'

'Is that such a bad thing?' He shrugged. 'Anyway, the word "control" sounds harsh. What I want is to be a good father.'

'And just have control of me?'

He smiled at that. 'Katie, I want control of you in a completely different way.'

His eyes slipped down over her curves and the air seemed to sizzle between them.

She knew exactly what he meant by that, and she remembered all too well how good it had felt to have him plundering her mouth, controlling her body...

'We are good together, Katie,' he told her softly. 'And do you really want our child to grow up meeting the different partners who just pass through our lives and yet ultimately affect his?'

Instinctively she put a protective hand down over her stomach as the words echoed through her consciousness. That was the very last thing she wanted. That was the situation that haunted her worst nightmares. For a moment she remembered some of her mother's men friends who had visited for a few weeks and then left. She remembered one in particular who had taken a dislike to her.

'Katie?' Alexi frowned as he saw how she paled suddenly.

'You're right. I don't want that situation.' She whispered the words unevenly.

'So let me take care of you both, hmm?' He reached out and tipped her chin up so that she was forced to meet his gaze.

The gentleness of that request simmered through her. She noticed how the suit he wore accentuated his powerful physique, how the white shirt brought out his Mediterranean skin tones, how dark his hair looked against the evening sky. He was so familiar to her. She knew him. She knew he meant it when he said he would care for her and for their child...

'I can give you everything you could ever wish for, Katie,' he said softly.

Except love, and she wanted that from him so desperately. The knowledge filtered through her uncomfortably.

Why? Why did that matter so much to her? Surely the most important thing was that their child would have a happy and secure upbringing?

Because she loved him. For a moment the truth was illuminated inside her as if a spotlight had been switched on inside her soul. That was why she had been so frightened of getting too close to him. That was why she was still running scared!

Every man she had ever known in her life had hurt her. And Alexi was capable of doing the most damage of all. Not physically—but emotionally. And the scars he could inflict would go much deeper than anything else.

Unrequited love was a difficult emotion to solve—Katie had tried to end the pain by severing the connections, but that hadn't worked. And now she was in even deeper. How could she sever the connections with the father of her child?

Even if she said no to his marriage proposal he would always be in the background of her life.

'I need your answer now, Katie—what is it to be?'

She pulled away from the touch of his hand.

He sounded so supremely confident. She hated that about him…yet loved that about him.

If she said no, would she regret it for the rest of her life? She had a sudden vision of the future—of watching Alexi's life from afar, seeing him at their child's school open-days, birthdays…

Her emotions twisted. Wasn't being with him better than not? And ultimately her child's welfare had to come first.

'OK!' The word was just a cautious whisper, but Alexi felt a fierce thrust of euphoria that was better than any multi-million-pound deal he'd accomplished after months of wrangling. She would be his.

'You've got a deal,' she continued before she could allow doubt to dissuade her. 'But only on my terms,' she added quickly. She couldn't allow him to take her over; she needed to remain strong. 'We'll have a long engagement, and—'

'No, we will not!' He cut across her firmly. He wasn't going to allow her to wriggle away from him again. 'It's my terms or nothing—my way or nothing.'

'Alexi!' Her heart was thundering against her chest now; she didn't like the steel in his voice, in his eyes.

'I've arranged for Captain Roberto to marry us here on board the *Octavia* before we leave for Greece tomorrow.'

'Hold on a moment—'

'No, Katie! You will play the dutiful wife, you will do everything that I ask of you, and in return I will treat you with respect and generosity: those are the terms.'

The terms hurt, they stung through her system like strong alcohol over a deep cut. 'I'm not a possession, Alexi!'

'Yet.' He reached and took hold of her wrists and gently moved her closer towards him. 'But I want to possess you, Katie…over and over and over again.'

She looked up and saw the fierce light of passion in his eyes, yet instead of pulling away she wanted to move closer.

OK, he didn't love her, but he did want her…he did crave her. And right now as he leaned closer and captured her lips with a fierce, possessive hunger she knew that would have to be enough—because she was incapable of saying no to him.

And maybe she loved him enough for the two of them.

She returned his kisses with equal passion, winding her arms up and around his neck. She didn't want to need him like this—but she did. So all that was left to her now was surrender.

She was breathless and shaking when he released her. The silence between them was filled by the sound of the party, the babble of conversation and music, and the rapid, thundering beat of her heart.

'I want you, Katie.' His voice was hard with desire. He stroked a finger over her skin, and it sent a million butterflies fluttering inside her. 'But we'll do this right. Tonight you will sleep alone here, on board ship. And then tomorrow we will consummate our marriage.'

A member of staff walked over towards them, interrupting them, and Katie took the opportunity to break away.

'Sir, we are about ready for the firework display. Do you want to say a few words before we proceed?'

Alexi glanced over and nodded. 'I'll be along in a moment,' he said dismissively.

They were left alone again, and for a few moments neither spoke.

A cool breeze whispered across her skin. She was scared, truly scared, by the speed with which things were progressing and by the emotions racing inside her. 'Alexi, we have over six months before the baby is born.'

'And we are going to use that time to get to know each other.' His eyes drifted down over her body. 'To enjoy each other again…'

She tried not to be turned on by the heat in his eyes and in his voice—tried to tell herself that she wasn't going to allow him to treat her like a sex object. But her body was sending conflicting signals to her brain. Her body was telling her that she wanted him and that it *was* a matter of great urgency.

He smiled as he saw the answering flame in her eyes. 'Tomorrow you will belong to me again, Katie.' He said the words with soft emphasis. 'The chapel is booked for three-thirty tomorrow. And after the service we will fly to Greece for a few days' honeymoon and a lot of catching up.'

Before she could get her breath to reply to that, he was walking away from her.

Katie turned and leaned against the ship's rail as she tried to gather herself together. She stared down at the water, at the glittering reflected lights from the ship and from the island of Manhattan as they danced and blurred on its silky darkness.

Had she done the right thing, accepting Alexi's proposal? She wanted him so much. Too much...

A breeze whispered against the heat of her skin, and she shivered violently and turned her back on the sea.

The party was heating up. There were about a hundred guests milling about on the deck, and the band was playing a rhythmic number.

She saw Alexi making his way purposefully through the assembled crowds. He looked very confident and in control as he stopped by the stage area and spoke to the string quartet who had set up ready to take over from the band later.

Then he took a mike someone handed him and, as the band finished their session and a round of applause broke out, the compère for the evening brought him up on stage.

He was greeted with wild applause and a lot of cheering, which made Katie smile.

Everyone liked Alexi, she thought wryly. He was a ruthlessly tough businessman, yet he had a way with people. She supposed it was because he was always fair, always straight. You knew where you stood with him.

She wished she didn't. She almost wished that he had lied

to her and told her he was falling in love with her. But then that wouldn't be Alexi! She bit down on her lip. And she didn't want to be treated like a fool, she told herself hastily.

'Ladies and gentlemen, I'd just like to welcome you all here tonight and thank you for coming. Also a big thank-you to everyone who has worked so hard to make sure *Octavia* was finished on time and to such high specifications.'

A big cheer went up from the crowd at that.

'Also, I would like to announce my engagement to Katie. A few of you might know Katie; she worked as Project Manager at Demetri Shipping for a few months, and now is with me at Madison Brown. She has consented to become my wife, and we will be married here on board *Octavia* tomorrow.'

The crowd broke into wild applause, and a spotlight circled, searching for her, and then caught her in its bright beam as everyone turned and clapped.

Katie was mortified. Why had he announced their wedding like this?

The spotlight faded away as Alexi continued swiftly. 'It just leaves me to say that I hope you enjoy the evening. The fireworks are about to commence, so take your places and raise your glasses to *Octavia*. The next piece of music to be played is for my wife-to-be...for Katie.'

As he finished speaking, a string quartet started to play a classical number. The heartrendingly beautiful music swelled and resonated through the night air, holding everyone spellbound.

It was one of Katie's favourite pieces of music. A piece that always made her feel emotional.

She remembered telling Alexi that once when it had been playing on a CD in her apartment.

She was surprised that he remembered.

Damn man! She blinked away the sudden tears that sprang to her eyes and moved away from the crowds that were milling around her.

Suddenly she needed to be on her own.

It wasn't hard to find space and dark solitude towards the front of the ship. She watched as golden fireworks exploded out over the water and showers of glitter rained down over the darkness.

'So, what do you think?' Alexi's voice close to her ear startled her, and she looked round and found herself too close to him.

'I was a bit taken aback by the announcement!'

'May as well tell people before the gossips get hold of it.'

'I suppose so.' She shrugged.

'We forgot something earlier,' he said suddenly.

'Did we?' She looked at him with a frown.

He reached into his pocket and took out a small square box. 'I went shopping this afternoon and bought this, just in case.'

He opened the lid, and the large, square diamond inside sparkled as it caught the reflection from the fireworks.

'It's beautiful, Alexi!' She looked up at him, her words tremulous. 'You obviously didn't have many doubts that I would say yes, did you?'

He shrugged. 'I thought common sense would prevail.'

It was strange—the setting was so romantic, the ring was perfect, and he was the man of her dreams...yet she still felt like her heart was breaking.

CHAPTER NINE

THE first thing Katie saw when she opened her eyes that morning was her engagement ring. It sparkled brightly in the early-morning sun, turning fire-gold and blue as she moved her hand.

It was her wedding day—she was going to marry Alexander Demetri! The knowledge crackled inside her with all the force of an electrical current. It was all happening too fast. The confirmation of her pregnancy, and now this. She felt confused, as if she were in the middle of some roller-coaster ride that twisted and turned until she was completely disorientated. All she was waiting for now was its final downward, cataclysmic spin.

But maybe that wouldn't happen, she told herself as she threw the covers of the bed back and got up. She couldn't go through with today if she didn't ultimately believe that things were going to work out.

Late last night as she'd climbed into bed she had phoned her sister to tell her the news. Lucy had been dumbstruck for a few moments.

'Just because you are pregnant it doesn't mean you have to get married!' she'd spluttered. 'I know our childhood was the pits, but you can't let the past cloud your judgement for the future.'

'Lucy, I'm being practical,' she had told her sister calmly. 'Bringing up a child alone will be difficult—for one thing my financial situation isn't great; I'm still paying a huge mortgage on my flat. And Alexi is more or less demanding that we should get married. He wants this child. And he is a very powerful, influential man.'

'You mean he is blackmailing you into marriage!'

Katie thought about that now for a moment as she looked at her reflection in the mirror. Then she looked about her. In the corner was a new suitcase filled with everything she would need for a few days in Greece. Hanging inside the wardrobe was a selection of new suits for her to choose from for the wedding ceremony.

Everything had been waiting for her when she had returned down here last night. Including the nightgown she was now wearing.

She didn't feel blackmailed, she felt as if she had been purchased, she thought wryly. As if Alexi was treating her like some concubine who was to be kept for his pleasure. Everything felt out of her hands...out of her control.

Alexi always got what he wanted, and he wanted her. But only because of the baby. Those were the facts.

It wasn't too late to change her mind; the thought stole, unwelcome, into her head.

But the trouble was that she didn't want to change her mind. She wanted to marry Alexi because she loved him.

She'd admitted as much to her sister before they had gone much further in the conversation last night, and Lucy had immediately relaxed.

'Why didn't you say so? That's different!'

She hadn't told her sister however that the feelings weren't reciprocated, that Alexi just wanted his baby. The truth had been too painful to disclose even to a person as dear to her and close to her as Lucy.

She had her pride.

She felt sick suddenly and had to rush towards the *en suite* bathroom.

Wedding-day nerves or morning sickness? she wondered. *Was she doing the right thing?*

That question had kept her awake for most of the night, and it was still zinging around inside her as she showered and then studied the clothes that had been sent down for her. The suits were all very stylish, plain, cream designer creations.

She settled on the first one she tried on because she honestly didn't have the energy for any more decision-making. It looked good on her anyway; the jacket had a cute design with a heart-shaped neckline, and it was teamed with a straight shift-dress that flattered her shapely figure. It was formal yet low key, which seemed to be in keeping with the situation.

Someone knocked on the door just as she was putting the finishing touches to her hair and make-up, and immediately her nerves swirled in panic in case it was Alexi. It was still early! Hastily she checked the security monitor, but it was just a florist delivering a bouquet.

They were beautiful flowers, pink roses and orchids swirled in a hand-tied design. As she closed the door again she read the accompanying card:

Thought you should have some flowers to accompany you down the aisle. See you at three.
Alexi.

He couldn't even write a lie on his card, she thought dryly, couldn't even write the words '*love*, Alexi'.

Not that it mattered, she told herself firmly. It was better this way, better that he should be honest. She took a deep breath of the flower's sweet perfume, trying to calm her nerves.

There was another knock at the door and she swung it open, expecting it to be some other delivery person. But this time it was Alexi who stood outside. He looked intensely and almost broodingly handsome in a dark formal suit, so much so that she could feel her system going into meltdown as soon as their eyes connected.

'You're early!' she said huskily. 'Your card said three! Are you checking up on me in case I become the runaway bride?' She tried to make a joke, but her voice didn't sound entirely steady.

'Is that how you feel?'

She shrugged. 'I feel like I'm in a bit of a daze, to be honest. It's all happening too fast.'

His lips twisted into an attractive half-smile. 'If it helps, I feel a bit like that, too.'

'Is that why we are doing this so fast? In case you are tempted to change your mind?' She frowned as the sudden thought struck her.

'I'm not going to change my mind, Katie,' he told her solemnly.

She felt a prickle of awareness as his eyes slowly swept over her appearance. 'We're doing this so fast because of the baby…and because we need time to be together and to adjust to living together before our child comes along.'

He made it all sound so practical, except for the way he

was looking at her, as if he were slowly undressing her with his eyes.

'You look lovely, by the way,' he told her as their eyes connected again.

'Thanks.' She felt shy for a moment…shy and awkward.

'So, are you going to let me come in?' He asked with a smile. 'Or are we going to stand out here in the corridor discussing our life?'

'Sorry.' She stepped back and allowed him to enter.

'There is some paperwork you need to sign before we proceed,' he said casually as he walked past her, and she noticed for the first time that he was carrying a folder.

'I thought that the paperwork was signed after the ceremony,' she said cautiously as she watched him spread the papers out on the table.

'It's just a standard prenuptial agreement,' he told her nonchalantly. 'Nothing heavy.'

She stared at him, her heart thundering uneasily against her chest. 'I see.'

'Don't look at me like that, Katie. Obviously we have to have a prenuptial. It's a prerequisite for company law-yers to protect the business.'

'And the business has to come first.' She tried to keep her voice flippant, but she was really hurting inside now. He couldn't have reinforced the cool pragmatism of this marriage any better if he'd taken out a notice in the trading index of the *Financial Times*.

'It's an unavoidable practicality.'

'Of course.' She tried very hard to sound as if she didn't care.

'So, are you going to sign on the bottom line or not?'

'Do I have a choice?'

'No.' He leaned back against the table and crossed his arms. 'But read it carefully, and if you want something changed we'll discuss it.'

'There's not much time for that, is there?' She glanced at her watch.

'It's a straightforward contract, Katie. With your knowledge of contracts, it will take you ten minutes to read.'

'And one minute for you to tell me it's non-negotiable. I've seen you in action in the boardroom, don't forget.'

He smiled at that. 'We know each other so well.'

When she didn't say anything to that he reached out and caught hold of her arms to draw her closer. 'I'm sure you'll find its terms acceptable.' His fingers stroked lightly down over her arm. 'I'm providing you with a more than generous allowance for as long as you remain married to me.'

The gentleness of his caress seemed almost insulting whilst he was talking about finance. Yet to her consternation his touch still made her come alive with a need she didn't want, with a desire she was desperate to curb.

'So it's a kind of payment for services rendered, you mean?' She slanted her chin up defiantly, but inside her emotions were fragmenting with the knowledge of what those services were.

'Now who's being cynical?' He raised one eyebrow.

'But it's true, isn't it?'

'If that's how you want to look at it.' His voice was cool. 'I just think it's for the best that we get everything sorted out, and then we can get on with our wedding—and with our life together.'

For a moment his gaze lingered on her lips. The look sent a yearning need spiralling through her.

She pulled away from him, furious with herself. 'Well, I suppose I better read it, then.'

Alexi watched calmly as she flicked through the pages, and his eyes drifted down over her body. Her figure was curvaceously enticing in the tight little suit. He couldn't wait to get her out of it...

'Unfortunately we are going to have to leave for the airport almost immediately after the wedding service,' he murmured. 'It's a long flight to Athens, so we will have to have our wedding breakfast on board. But on the plus side we will arrive in Athens at a reasonable time of day.'

'I don't know why we are bothering going to Greece anyway,' she said crisply, trying to sound as businesslike as him. 'Pretending that we need a romantic honeymoon just seems absurd! We both know that this marriage is just a convenient arrangement, nothing more.'

'That doesn't mean we can't enjoy ourselves.' He smiled. 'It's only a short break, but I think it's appropriate somehow that our first few days and nights of love-making as man and wife should be in Greece.'

The words were dangerously tantalising. And she suddenly wondered how she was going to maintain this cool, pragmatic pretence when he finally did take her into his arms to claim her as his wife. The very thought made her burn inside with trepidation. If she wanted to be left with any scrap of pride or dignity, she was going to have to try. So she flicked him a glance from shimmering blue eyes and strove for some dismissive kind of reply. 'You mean, where better to consummate things than in the hub of your business empire?'

He just smiled at that. 'Indeed!'

Katie picked up the pen he had left next to the documents and for a few moments she hesitated.

Could she really do this? The question niggled persistently. Could she really pretend that her feelings weren't involved? That her emotions weren't in turmoil?

But not being with him was going to be worse, she reminded herself bleakly. And she had a child to consider.

With a shaking hand she signed her name quickly on both pages. 'There.' She turned to face him. 'Now you've got what you want.'

'Not quite, Katie. But nearly,' he told her, his eyes warm with a promise that made her blood turn to fire.

The roar of the jet increased as the pilot brought the aircraft down from thirty-thousand feet to circle the skies above Athens, ready for landing.

Alexi folded his papers away and looked across towards Katie. She was in the seat opposite, and she had been fast asleep for several hours.

Hardly surprising, he thought. Their time in New York had been eventful to say the least. He found himself remembering the shimmering vulnerability in her blue eyes as he had placed the wedding band on her finger in the chapel.

The wedding service itself had taken about twenty minutes, yet that one moment kept replaying over and over through his mind with an insistent force that was very disconcerting.

He didn't know why he should keep thinking about it because he had no doubts about this marriage whatsoever. He wanted this child with a fierce certainty, and he believed a child needed both parents. He also fervently wanted Katie in his bed. Marriage was the perfect solution.

He allowed his eyes to move leisurely over her flushed

countenance, taking in the soft curve of her lips and the dark, thick eyelashes. She looked so young and beautiful.

Suddenly her eyelashes flickered open and their eyes connected.

'Afternoon, sleepy head.' He smiled at her.

For a second she smiled back, a warm, sleepy smile that reminded him of the way she'd looked at him the very first time they had ever made love.

He remembered he'd gone over to her apartment on the pretext of discussing work. But they had both known that the work was secondary to the desire that had been swirling between them in the office all day. One kiss had led to another, and suddenly he had been carrying her through to the bedroom. He'd stayed until the early hours of the morning and even then he hadn't wanted to leave. He hadn't been able to get enough of her.

He remembered her telling him how extraordinary she felt when she woke up and found him across the pillow from her. 'It's a bit like a dream,' she'd murmured.

'An X-certificate dream,' he'd laughed, and that had made her blush and get annoyed. And then he'd kissed her some more…

'What time is it?' she asked now, and he pulled his thoughts away from the provocative memories.

'Almost two-thirty, Greek time, we're waiting for clearance from air traffic control to land.'

'I can't believe I've slept so long!' She brought the chair back upright.

'It was a long flight, and you were obviously very tired.'

Katie nodded. Emotionally exhausted was how she felt; otherwise there would have been no way she would have conceded to sleep.

She swallowed hard as the memories of their wedding rushed through her mind. The ceremony had been so fast, and the number of people who had been there had surprised her. All of them had been employees, people who had just wanted to wish them well in their new life together, people who thought they were madly in love and told them that they made a perfect couple.

Katie had been painfully aware that Alexi looked mildly amused by some of the comments, and she had felt completely self-conscious. Especially when Alexi had kissed her at the end of the ceremony and everyone had applauded.

The thought of that kiss made her grow hot all over again; it had been extremely sensual. She had thought, when they'd got on board the company jet to leave, that he would have kissed her again…but he hadn't. In fact there were staff on board, and they had been served a delightful meal sitting at a table laid with the finest silverware.

It all felt somehow bizarre.

'You've been doing some work,' she noticed now as she looked across at the papers strewn out in front of him.

'Yes, I thought I would get it out of the way and then we can relax for the next couple of days and nights.'

The words flicked through her mind with disconcerting emphasis.

Alexi watched as she brushed a hand nervously over the cream suit, remembering the shy acquiescence of her kiss at the end of the wedding service.

So far it had taken all his self-control to keep his hands off her.

But he wanted the first time they made love as man and wife to be in Greece, for it to be special, leisurely…

'What's on the itinerary for the rest of the day?' she asked suddenly.

As soon as the question left her lips she regretted it as she saw the way his eyes swept over her figure.

'I'm going to take you home, take you out of that lovely little suit, and, well, just take you…and take you,' he murmured huskily.

The words made her cheeks glow with bright colour, and he smiled. 'You blush like a virgin, do you know that,' he told her teasingly.

'Well, I'm certainly not a virgin,' she told him gruffly. 'In fact anything but, considering my condition.'

'Ah, yes, how is Junior?' He smiled.

'OK. At least not making me feel ill…which is an improvement, considering how I felt first thing before our wedding.'

'Hopefully he will behave himself for the next few months and allow you to relax.'

Katie didn't feel like she would ever be able to relax again. Her eyes flicked back to the paperwork open in front of him.

'I don't know about that. I have a stack of work to get through in the next few months. I should be doing some now, too.'

Alexi laughed. 'It's OK, you're with the boss, you can play hooky with impunity—at least for the next few days.'

She smiled.

'And if you are not up to continuing with your work, Katie, you only need to say. I'll find someone else to take over from you.'

'Of course I'm up to it!' She looked at him in consternation. She needed to keep busy…and she needed to keep her independence. 'And I intend to keep working even after our baby is born,' she told him firmly.

Alexi shrugged. 'That's up to you,' he said. 'But there is no need, I assure you.'

'Well, I think there is.' She looked at him pointedly. 'I think there is every need for me to be completely independent from you financially. I don't even want that allowance you have drawn up for me—I don't want anything from you.'

He raised an eyebrow at that.

'I mean it, Alexi.' Her voice shook slightly. 'I don't want your charity.'

'Charity?' He frowned. 'Katie, you're my wife and the mother of my child,' he told her softly. 'Charity doesn't come into this. I want you to be well taken care of.'

'I can take care of myself!' she maintained stiffly.

For a moment Alexi watched her, puzzled by the fierceness of her stance. Now he came to think about it, her attitude had always been one of very determined self-reliance. He'd admired her for it in the past, but now he started to wonder at its root cause. What was behind that vulnerable need to be completely in control of her life?

'As your husband I *want* to protect you, Katie. And I can afford to keep you,' he added teasingly.

'No need—but thanks.' Her smile was over-bright for a moment. Yes, he wanted to protect her and care for her now, because she was carrying his child, but what happened if the pregnancy went wrong—if she lost the baby? The idea swirled suddenly in her mind. It was very early days, anything could happen! And if she did lose the baby would he suddenly be suggesting a quickie divorce? She wouldn't be surprised.

All the more reason to remain as independent and as emotionally strong as she could, she told herself firmly.

Silence fell between them, and Katie glanced out of the window. The sky was a clear cobalt-blue, and below she could see the glitter of the sea and the gentle curve of the Greek coastline. It looked like a gloriously hot day.

She wondered if Alexi would be taking her to his apartment in Athens. He'd told her about it, but she had never visited. Her one and only trip to Athens had been strictly work-related. Although he had taken her out to lunch, she'd spent most of the time with him at the offices and then she had jetted straight back to London alone because Alexi had been going to visit one of his younger sisters who'd just had a baby.

Katie remembered that she'd told herself at the time that she hadn't wanted to accompany him, hadn't wanted to meet his family. But deep down she admitted now that she had been disappointed he hadn't extended an invitation.

The memory made a curl of hurt stir somewhere deep inside.

The pilot's voice interrupted her thoughts. 'We have clearance for landing, Mr Demetri. Ten minutes.'

She would have to stop thinking about the past. OK, Alexi hadn't thought enough of her to introduce her to his family, but now she *was* his family!

It was the future that mattered, not the past…and maybe one day Alexi would grow to love her.

As she looked across at him that hope shimmered inside. It was the only thing keeping her positive. 'So, where are we going to stay whilst we are here?'

'I own a house out near my parents' place. I thought we would spend our few days there.'

'Fine.' She shrugged.

'It's been sitting empty for a while, but I rallied some cleaning staff, and it should be aired for us.'

The engine noises were accelerating again, and Katie could feel a weightless sensation in the pit of her stomach as the plane started to descend, and she started to think again about the night ahead.

CHAPTER TEN

UNLIKE previous trips there was no limousine waiting for them at the airport. Instead Alexi headed for the car park where he picked up a shiny, red convertible sportscar.

'Is this yours?' Katie asked as she settled herself into the luxurious cream leather seats.

'Of course.' He tossed their luggage in the boot and shot her a look of amusement. 'I always keep a car here. When I'm not working I like to drive.'

'And I bet that doesn't happen very often,' she said sardonically.

'Not as often as I'd like, no.'

Alexi flicked a button and the roof started to go back. Katie lifted her face to the sultry rays of sun.

'So have you always been a workaholic, or is it something that just fell upon you in your thirties?' she asked as they drove out of the airport and joined a busy main road.

He laughed at that. 'I suppose I've always enjoyed my work too much. I find it exciting and challenging, and certainly after my divorce I decided it was possibly even more rewarding than a social life.'

She stared out at the passing countryside and silence fell between them.

'How about you?' he asked her suddenly. 'Have you always been a workaholic?'

'I guess I'm the same as you, only without the divorce bit,' she added jokingly, and then smiled over at him. 'I like a challenge.'

'So that guy—the one who hurt you—what exactly happened?' Alexi asked suddenly.

The unexpectedly personal question made her hesitate.

'It just didn't work.' Her reply was measured, 'I thought he was serious about me...but it turned out I was wrong.'

Although she said the words lightly, Alexi sensed that her feelings ran a little deeper than that.

'And you loved him?'

Katie bit down on her lip. She'd thought she loved him, but she realised now that the feelings she'd had for Carl hardly scraped the surface of what she felt for Alexi.

Aware that he was waiting for a reply, she just shrugged. 'It doesn't really matter now, does it?'

'No, I suppose not.' Alexi concentrated on the road again.

It shouldn't matter, but strangely it did, and that made anger twist inside him. What the hell was the matter with him? he wondered. He wasn't the type to get jealous, he never had been, and he never would be. He didn't do those kinds of emotions. The guy was history, anyway; Katie belonged to him now. Maybe lack of sex was affecting his brain, he thought wryly. Over a month of abstinence had obviously taken its toll, and now he needed to play catch-up with his body's demands. Some undisturbed time in the bedroom...in the lounge...in the kitchen...wherever and whenever he wanted her...should just about do the trick. He smiled to himself.

He changed down gears. The scenery was softening.

They were on a winding coast road where the tree-covered mountains tumbled down to meet the Mediterranean. Every now and then there was a glimpse of a deserted white-gold beach.

Silence settled between them again.

'It's beautiful here,' she reflected.

'Yes.' He pulled off the road suddenly and parked in a lay-by that gave a view down along the coast.

Her heart bounced unsteadily until she realised he'd stopped to take a phone call.

She tried to relax back into the leather seats. The heat of the afternoon was intense. Alexi was speaking in Greek. She found his voice incredibly sexy; it washed over her like the day, hot, languid and intensely pleasurable.

Her eyes drifted down over the coastline; there was a yacht with white sails skipping out over the blue of the sea, and just at the curve of the bay she could see a house nestling amidst the greenery of the hillside. It was painted white and had a red-tiled roof.

Alexi finished his call and followed her gaze. 'What do you think of the house?'

'It's beautiful,' she murmured.

'Well, I'm glad you like it, because it belongs to me, and it's where I would like to set up home with you.'

The husky words caused a flame of emotion to flare up inside of her. 'It looks very big! I thought you liked con-dominiums and sleek bachelor-pads in the hub of things.'

'I do. But now I'm going to become a family man...' He smiled at her. 'And my priorities have changed.'

The sentiment sounded good, so good that she found herself swallowing hard on the knot in her throat as she desperately tried to keep herself grounded in reality. Alexi was doing all this because of the baby, not because of her…and she had to remember that!

'Of course, if you want to continue with your career you might find it a bit isolated—but we can work around that. You can commute to Athens from here.'

'I might have to learn Greek first!'

'Well, I can certainly help you with that,' he murmured huskily. 'I think a few private lessons could be arranged.' His eyes were on her lips as he spoke.

She could feel the heat in that look—almost as warm as the day itself. If only he had real feelings for her, she thought longingly. If only this was real. She almost wished that the first pregnancy test she'd done had come back positive and he'd proposed back then, because at least she wouldn't have had the cold proof that without it he'd just let her go…

He re-started the car engine and she tried to let go of the thoughts—they weren't helping.

The driveway to the house was hidden amongst a riot of greenery. They turned through the entrance and drove down past manicured gardens. Then as they rounded a corner the house opened out in front of them in spectacular style. It looked even larger up close, and the views out across the sea were breathtaking.

Katie stepped out into the warmth of the afternoon and looked up at it in wonder. She had never thought that she would live somewhere like this. 'The whole of my flat would probably fit into a tiny corner of one room here!' she murmured.

'Well, you don't need your flat any more. You may as well put it up for sale.'

Katie didn't think she would rush into that—her flat felt

like a safety net that she was loathe to let go of—but she said nothing as she followed Alexi up the steps to the front door.

'As it's tradition, I should carry you over the threshold,' Alexi said assertively.

The thought of him touching her made her senses dissolve. 'I don't think there is any need for that! We're hardly a traditional couple, are we—?'

Before she had even finished speaking he had swung her up into his arms. Caught off-guard she was forced to put her hands on his shoulders to hold on to him. She could smell the familiar tang of his aftershave, could feel the heat of his body against hers, the power of his muscles beneath her fingertips.

Being in his arms brought back a flood of memories. She remembered the first time they had made love in her flat. She remembered the feelings, the exquisite tenderness of his touch combined with the almost ruthless domination of her body.

She wanted to lean in against him and wind her arms more tightly around his neck, wanted to give in to the yearning need he stirred inside her. It took all her self-control to hold herself stiff and unyielding against him. 'Are you going to put me down now?' she asked as they crossed the hallway.

'Definitely not!' He continued on up the curving stairway and along the galleried landing.

Her heart was racing against her chest as he pushed a door open and then placed her down inside the bedroom.

For a moment she stood awkwardly in front of him, and his eyes seemed to burn with intensity as he looked at her.

'Well, Mrs Demetri, this is exactly where I have wanted you all day…where I have pictured you all day…' He traced a finger down over the side of her face and then traced it lower to the sweetheart neckline, teasing her with the butterfly caress. 'In fact, maybe for longer than that...'

Katie swallowed the raw feeling in her throat. This was exactly where she had been picturing herself all day, too. She wanted him so much, but she was also frightened— frightened of revealing her true feelings for him, and of giving her heart and soul to him only for it to be smashed to smithereens if this fragile marriage fell apart.

His hand moved from the side of her neck to her face, stroking it gently, whilst his thumb held her chin so that she was forced to look up at him. 'This is what your eyes have been asking of me ever since you walked back into my office.'

'You are the most arrogant and conceited man I have ever met, Alexi!' Her voice trembled, but not as much as her body as his other hand moved to unfasten the top button of her jacket.

He noticed the subtle yet unmistakable way she quivered as his fingers brushed against her skin, noticed the way her nipples hardened against the cream silk material.

He smiled to himself as a flare of triumph soared through him. For all her prickly defences, the chemistry was still scorching between them. He knew it and so did she.

Katie could feel her heart thundering against her breast. His lips were just centimetres from hers, and she wanted him to kiss her. Wanted it so much that her whole body ached.

Desperately she tried to counteract the feelings. 'If you must know, I haven't looked at you with anything but distrust since I walked back into your office.' She forced herself to say the words; she couldn't allow him to think for one moment that her heart was his. She had to keep strong; she had to remember that he had allowed her to walk away from him, that he hadn't wanted a real relationship with her until the baby.

He laughed at that. 'So that morning at my apartment was just a figment of my imagination?'

Her skin flared with bright embarrassment as she remembered how much she had wanted him. How dared he mention that and laugh at her? 'Sometimes I—I don't even like you!' she muttered angrily.

'Don't you?' He smiled, but his eyes narrowed. 'But you like what my body can do for you, you always have.' His fingers skimmed over her breasts, caressing them through the silk, and she closed her eyes on a wave of immediate ecstasy.

He leaned closer and his lips covered hers hungrily and possessively, his body pressing hard against hers.

This was where she wanted to be—it was the only place to be—in his arms, his lips hungrily devouring her. She kissed him back, her hands moving upwards to stroke along the broad contours of his muscular torso.

'You see?' He pulled away from her and smiled. 'Katie, you can pretend as much as you want, but we both know that we are good together, and you still want me so badly it hurts.'

As he spoke he trailed a hand down over the collar of her dress. Then he started to take off her jacket and allowed it to fall to the floor.

Her breathing felt tight with a mixture of apprehension and desire.

'And you belong to me now...' The arrogant words inflamed her senses, as did the touch of his lips against her neck as he pulled her closer.

She leaned against him weakly, loving the feel of his

body against hers, the familiar scent of him, the possessive touch of his hands circling her waist.

He started to unfasten the buttons at the back of her dress until it fell from her shoulders. She put a hand up, trying to catch it, but he brushed her hand away.

Then he pulled the dress down so that it slithered to the floor, and she stood before him in her lacy bra and pants.

His eyes raked over her body. God, but she was gorgeous. She'd lost a little weight since they'd last made love, but her body was still perfect. Her breasts were pushed up, high and pert above the band of her bra; her waist was tiny, her hips gently curved. Just looking at her gave him a thrill of pleasure beyond belief.

'You are so beautiful, Katie.'

The warmth of his eyes on her body, and the guttural sound of his voice, made her melt inside. She wanted him so much.

His hands moved upwards, roughly stroking against her breasts through the lace material. 'There's so much that's unfinished between us...'

She moved her head to find his lips, and as they met it felt like barriers were crashing down inside her like huge steel gates of emotion. She groaned with pleasure as his hand moved to push down her bra, his thumbs stroking over her with a sensual heat that made her gasp with desire.

She closed her eyes as his hands squeezed against her, toying with her, then he lowered his head and his lips took one hard, throbbing peak into the warmth of his mouth.

She quivered with arousal, and the last of her control snapped completely. Her hands raked through the darkness of his hair, then her nails scratched down the powerful lines of his back through his shirt as she pressed herself closer, her need for him like a burning fever.

'Ah… My little wild Kat has come back!' He laughed with pleasure as he scooped her up into his arms and put her down on the bed.

Then he straddled her, kissing her, stroking her, teasing her with his tongue until she was panting and wild for him. She reached to try and unfasten the buttons on his shirt, her hands trembling and unsteady.

He helped her and the shirt was thrown to the floor. For a second her eyes moved over his powerful torso. 'You have a perfect body,' she murmured, tracing one hand over the satin-smooth shoulders that gleamed like gold in the afternoon sunlight slanting through the window beside them.

He laughed at that. 'You've stolen my lines,' he whispered as his hands curved against her breasts, his fingers squeezing against her nipples until they pulsated, heavy with pleasure and need.

She closed her eyes on a wave of ecstasy.

'You like that, hmm?'

She could hear the teasing gleam of enjoyment in his voice.

His hands stroked lower over her ribs and down over her pants, finding the core of her and then tormenting her through the delicate silk.

She groaned with pleasure as his caress became firmer, more insistent.

Katie couldn't think of anything now except the pleasure he could give her, and the aching void inside her. 'Alexi, I want you so much.' The words were torn from her.

And then he pulled away from her.

'Where are you going?' Her eyes snapped open in panic and he laughed.

'I'm not going anywhere, believe me.' He'd been holding on to his control by a whisper, but now that she was truly ready for him he was going to savour this moment. He unbuckled his belt and took off his trousers.

'Tell me again how much you want me,' he commanded softly as he took off his boxers.

'You know how much I want you,' she whispered unevenly, and he noticed the way she moistened her lips and looked at him with those playful come-to-bed eyes.

He found himself hardening so much that he was uncomfortable now.

Unable to bear it a moment longer, he reached for her, pulling her down against him. 'I've missed you so much, Katie.'

The murmured words gave her a thrill of pleasure unlike any other as he rained kisses down over her face before crushing his lips against hers.

She gasped with joy as he rolled her over, tipping her head back, raking his hands through her hair, pulling it roughly as his lips nuzzled in against her neck. The sensation was pure sensual bliss.

'I don't know how I've waited this long to have you again.' His mouth was on hers again now, his tongue entering the softness of her mouth, taking possession as his hands moved over the narrow curve of her waist, then lower to push down the flimsy pants that she wore.

She felt him push deep inside her and she cried out in rapture, running her hands over the broad, smooth contours of his back as she drew him as close to her as she possibly could.

He smiled. 'This is the Katie I remember so well, the Kat I like to play with, torment and tease...' He laced the words with kisses along her neck, and she shuddered with delight, wrapping her legs around him, holding him tight and giving herself up to the thrill of his body.

Alexi felt lost as soon as he entered her—he wanted her with a force that was overwhelming in its intensity. He felt like he'd been starved of her and now had to gorge on her, take her and take her and drive himself into her, with thrusting, deep strokes until they became absolutely one.

He spoke to her in Greek, forgetting everything, forgetting almost who he was in the mist of his desire.

And she matched his passion, her body merging with his with a wanton, passionate disregard for everything but the moment.

Katie cried out his name as she exploded inside with long, shuddering, orgasmic pleasure. He followed soon after, and she held him tightly against her body, absorbing the shudders of his body, stroking her hands caressingly over his shoulders, turning her mouth to find his lips and drink him in.

For a long while afterwards they just lay closely entwined—exhausted. Alexi's body was hot against hers, his arms like tight bands of possession around her. She cuddled closer, loving the feeling of warmth and closeness. She'd missed him so much. She wanted to cry at the sheer pleasure of being held in his arms again. And the fact that he'd told her he'd missed her swirled pleasurably with the sated, exhausted threads of her emotions.

Maybe this marriage would work. Maybe there was a chance for them. Maybe he would start to fall in love with her…

After all, in the right situations, love could be nurtured and cultivated until it blossomed like a flower.

He pressed a kiss against her forehead and she smiled, drowsily contented.

Alexi pulled away from her slightly, and his eyes drifted down over the warm curves of her body. He'd known he wanted her, but the extreme force of that need had taken him totally by surprise. He'd lost control—and that never happened to him.

He wanted her again, wanted her right now. The sudden need hit him again and it angered him. He didn't want to feel like this. He wanted to feel sated now, wanted the bewitching spell she had cast over him to abate so that he could take her again at his leisure when it suited him. He wanted absolute control over his emotions.

She rolled over and looked up at him with clear blue eyes. 'Tell me again that you missed me,' she whispered.

The question splintered through him.

'You know I've missed you. You're great in bed, Katie.'

He said the words with a frown, and they hit her like a physical whack of a stick.

The world had been held at bay whilst she was in his arms, and she'd believed him when he'd said he'd missed her. But what he'd really meant was that he had missed her body, nothing more. Would she never learn? How could she be so stupid? A hot wave of shame rushed through her as she remembered how hungrily and greedily she had needed him.

'Do you want a drink of something?' Alexi forced himself to move away from her.

'Some water would be good.' She reached hastily for her clothes on the floor and found her underwear. Her hands were shaking as she tried to fasten her bra.

Alexi watched her, momentarily distracted. He loved the

way she looked after sex, her hair all messed up and her skin flushed.

God, he wanted her.

'We'll make love again later,' he told her abruptly. He noticed how her hands weren't completely steady now as they flew to pick up her jacket, shutting out his view of her curves.

'I think I'll have a shower and get changed.'

Something about the way she looked over at him made him reach out and catch her arm before she could move away. 'Katie, are you OK?'

'Of course.' Her blue eyes shimmered for a moment, too wide, too impossibly blue for the pallor of her skin.

'I didn't hurt you, did I?'

For a moment the gentleness of that question threw her—and she thought he realised how she was feeling.

'I wasn't too rough?' he asked softly, and his eyes moved down over her to rest on her stomach, and she realised he was just worried about the baby.

'No—it was fine.' She moved away and came round to pick up her dress.

'Fine?' For a moment he frowned. 'I think it was more than fine.'

Her hair flowed like liquid silk around her shoulders as she glanced over at him. 'Not worried about your sexual prowess, are you, Alexi?' She couldn't resist the jibe—she was hurting inside, and she wanted to hurt him, too. Wanted to act and talk as if she didn't care. 'You were good,' she said airily. 'Don't concern yourself. It was more than…adequate.'

She knew she had gone too far when she saw his eyes darken. Alexi was used to being complimented in the bedroom, used to women idolising him. 'Adequate?' he asked.

She shrugged and tried to walk away, but he caught hold of her wrist again and pulled her back.

'Now run that by me again.' He pulled her down onto his knee. She looked very sexy in just her jacket and underwear, her long, bare legs shapely and inviting.

'Alexi, I'm going for a shower. I haven't got the energy to reassure you.'

'Very amusing, Katie!' He smiled at that. 'Well, let's see if we can conjure some energy up, shall we?' He pulled her closer and crushed her lips with his. For a moment she tried to resist him, tried to act as if his kiss meant little, but after a while the passion and the heat started to simmer inside her and she started to kiss him back hungrily.

'Now run that word by me again,' he murmured, his hand moving inside the jacket, stroking over her curves.

The way he was caressing her now made her scared that he could prove his point all too easily. 'Don't, Alexi. Stop…'

He pulled down her bra, stroking her breasts with firm strokes. 'Now what were you saying?' he asked playfully as he felt her body responding very positively.

What had she been saying? She couldn't remember. She couldn't remember anything except how good that was. 'Alexi, don't stop,' she whispered as his hand moved away.

'I've no intention of stopping…' he told her huskily. 'None at all.'

Katie lifted her head to the full force of the shower, letting it run over her face in cooling jets. After the heat of their passion she needed cooling down. How was it that Alexi was able to turn her on like that? How did he make her feel so alive, so excited—almost delirious with passion and then so sated—so deeply sated? And then so sad…

The first time they had made love had been wild and abandoned but just now he had taken her with a gentle tenderness that had been so incredibly moving it made her just want to cry.

But it was just sex, she reminded herself fiercely. Alexi had just been proving to her how much he could control her and turn her on. And the tenderness had been just out of deference to the fact that she was expecting their child.

There was no point reading anything into it. No point day dreaming or hoping for loving, meaningful words; it wasn't going to happen.

She snapped off the water, stepped out of the shower and put on one of the fluffy white-towelling robes that were hanging on the back of the door.

Then she stepped back through to the bedroom. Alexi had left about thirty minutes ago—but he must have returned whilst she'd been in the shower because their luggage was now sitting next to the wardrobe. She opened up her case and wondered what she should put on.

Alexi had said something about having an intimate candlelight supper out on the terrace. The thought made her heart tight with pain.

She had all the trappings of a romantic honeymoon—but none of the feelings. Was she destined to go through her marriage like this? Was this as good as it would get? And just say Alexi got tired of her soon? He enjoyed a challenge, and if he could have her twenty-four-seven then sexually he might want to move on to some other conquest. He might just keep her tidily tucked away in the background—the little wife who had given him the all-important heir.

She sat down on the bed. Why was she torturing herself with these thoughts? She needed to stop. She needed not to care!

Her eyes drifted around the room. Deep golden carpets covered the floor and turquoise-and-gold heavy curtains hung at windows leading out to a large balcony. The doors were open, and a soft breeze stirred the frothy voiles that were pulled across to keep the insects out.

Katie felt a little disorientated after all the travelling, and she would have liked to lie down and sleep, but, mindful of the fact that Alexi could come into the room at any moment, she got up and went to stand by the windows.

Night had descended with speed, and she could just make out the dark silhouettes of the cypress trees against the moonlit sky and the silvery glitter of the sea. She felt a little better after some deep breaths of the sea air. She could hear the sound of the cicadas, and the distant rush of the tide against the shore.

She would get dressed; she would face Alexi and she would act cool and reserved. OK, she couldn't act that way when he kissed her, when they made love, but she could manage it on a day-to-day basis. She had to keep strong if she was going to make this marriage work.

Katie rummaged through her case and found a floral summer dress in pastel shades. She tried it on and surveyed her reflection. Feminine yet sexy—just right, she thought with a nod.

She took her time blow-drying her hair and applying a light make-up.

It was almost nine when she stepped out of the bedroom and walked down the stairs.

The house was magnificent. A chandelier threw spar-kling light over the grand entrance-hall, and to either side there were reception rooms of breathtaking proportions, each opening out to a terrace that ran the length of the house. As she lingered by the doorway through to the first of the sitting rooms she saw that Alexi was on the terrace, looking out to sea. He seemed lost in thought.

What was he thinking about? Katie wondered. She wondered if this house held memories of his first wife...if they had lived here together.

She was going to move away but he turned and saw her. 'Come and join me,' he invited. 'It's a beautiful evening.'

Katie did as he asked. He was wearing black jeans and a black T-shirt, she noticed. He looked so handsome and strong and vital that her stomach twisted into knots. She would have given anything to stand close to him, reach for his hand. But she didn't dare. It was too possessive, too intimate, which seemed absurd after what they had just shared! But she had to resurrect barriers, she reminded herself sharply, had to play this situation carefully and protect herself.

He looked over at her and swiftly she glanced away. 'Fabulous view from out here,' she murmured, looking down over the sweep of a lawn that ran seamlessly down to a private beach and a jetty where a small yacht was anchored.

'Yes, it's a nice place.'

'Is the yacht yours?'

For a moment Alexi didn't reply; it was as if he were deep in thought.

'Alexi?' She glanced over at him again.

'Actually, I bought it for Andrea.' He turned his back on the view and gave her his full attention suddenly. 'She wanted to learn how to sail, but she didn't really take to the water—got bored with it after a while. I should get rid of it—I just haven't had the time.'

Or maybe he just didn't want to get rid of it, a little voice suggested inside Katie. Maybe the memories were too bittersweet to let go of it.

'You and Andrea lived here, then?' She tried to make her voice sound casual.

'For a few months, but she is a city girl, so we moved back into Athens.' He shrugged. 'Anyway, on a more interesting note, this house used to belong to my grandparents. They left it in perpetuity for me, my children and my children's children. I used to come here a lot as a boy.'

'It must have been an idyllic childhood.'

Alexi smiled. 'Yes, I was lucky. I'm from a large, very close family; it made my childhood feel very secure. That's what I want for our child.'

'That's what I want, too.' She tried to smile, but it felt decidedly shaky. She wanted that so much, it hurt.

'We've done the right thing, you know—getting married,' he told her suddenly.

She nodded, but deep down she wondered if he really meant that—or if he was trying to convince himself as much as her.

Alexi frowned as he noticed the flicker of distress in her blue eyes. 'We'll be happy—we'll work at it,' he told her softly.

Such sensible words, she thought with a sudden stab of anger. 'Yes, of course we'll work at it—and the fact that we don't love each other will somehow magically become acceptable.'

She probably shouldn't have said that. For a moment there was a tense silence between them and then he just shrugged. 'Well, we will just have to hope for the best, won't we?'

The phone was ringing inside the house. 'Excuse me, Katie—I better take that.'

She watched him walk away and then turned her attention to the view again. The yacht bobbed against its mooring, a little breeze whispering and whistling through the ropes that held her secure. Almost like the ghost of his first marriage, Katie thought wryly, laughing at her...

CHAPTER ELEVEN

THE phone call had been to invite them over to a party at Alexi's parents' house.

It was to be a large family celebration in honour of their wedding, and Katie was feeling more than a little apprehensive as they set off the next afternoon.

'Relax,' Alexi told her as they drove along the spectacular scenery of the winding coast road. 'There's nothing to worry about.'

He seemed to be finding the fact that she was edgy about this meeting rather amusing, she realised with annoyance.

'I thought you said they weren't happy about our marriage!' she retorted. 'Surely that is some cause for concern?'

'They are not unhappy because I got married, they are unhappy because I did it secretively—they would have liked to be there—they would have liked an almighty, great big, all-singing, all-dancing, Greek wedding, to be blunt.' Alexi changed down gears to take a very steep bend. 'But I did that first time around, and that kind of ceremony wasn't the right thing for us. They will accept that when I explain.'

'And how are you planning to explain?' Katie asked.

'Are you going to tell them that we're not really in love so there was no point having the big family wedding?'

'Of course not!' Alexi frowned and glanced over at her again. 'I'm going to tell them it was a whirlwind decision.'

'And are you going to tell them about the baby?' Her voice was husky.

'I was going to—yes.'

'Well, I'd rather you didn't. It's early days, Alexi, anything could happen. I mean really—sensibly speaking—we shouldn't have rushed into marriage at all, we should have waited until I was at least three months pregnant to be on the safe side. Or even waited until after the baby was born.'

He frowned. 'Katie, nothing is going to go wrong!'

'You don't know that!'

'I know that we've done the right thing. So chill out, OK? Getting so worked up isn't going to help Junior!'

She nodded and tried to relax back into the seat.

'And if it worries you I won't tell them about the baby,' he added softly. 'We'll wait until you feel the time is right.'

'Thanks.' She nodded. 'I think that would be for the best.'

Silence fell between them.

Alexi flicked a look over at her. She'd caught a little sun as they'd sat beside the pool this morning. She looked healthy and glowing in the white sundress, her lips moist with peach satin-gloss. Her dark hair glowed with chestnut lights, and lay silky-straight around her shoulders. Yet there was a look in her eyes that concerned him—a vulnerable look that he knew she tried quickly to hide as soon as he glanced in her direction.

She hadn't slept very well last night, either. She'd got

up as dawn was breaking and had got herself a glass of water from downstairs. Then she hadn't returned to the bedroom until he'd got up and was in the shower.

She'd said that she was suffering from jet lag—which was entirely feasible. Yet Alexi had a feeling that whatever was bothering her ran deeper than that.

Even when they had made love again last night he'd felt that she was holding herself back from him, somehow. Although her kisses had been passionate and needy, there had still been that underlying vulnerability about her.

Was she regretting their marriage? he wondered suddenly. Had he rushed her into something that was ultimately making her deeply unhappy?

He frowned. They had a child to consider, he reminded himself. She would come round. She would have to!

They arrived at Alexi's parents' house just as the sun was starting to go down and Katie would never forget her first glimpse of the place. The mansion was set in its own grounds with spectacular views across the sea. Behind the house the forests melted into the dusky pink of the twilight sky.

There were already a lot of cars lined up on the driveway, and light and music spilled out from the open front door.

'The party sounds like it's in full swing. Are we late?' Katie asked as they parked and stepped out into the warmth of the evening.

'No, we're on time. They probably wanted everyone here before us, so they could welcome you properly. I'll warn you now—I have enough aunts, uncles and cousins to repopulate the lost city of Atlantis,' he told her calmly. 'So don't worry if you can't remember names—or work out who everyone is—even I struggle sometimes,' he added with a smile.

Katie knew what he meant as they stepped inside. There were crowds of people milling about in the vast marble entrance-hall, and by the time they had reached the doors to the reception areas Alexi had introduced her to so many relatives, and she had been warmly hugged by so many strangers, that she had completely lost track of who was who.

Alexi's parents were out on the patio, organising a barbeque.

Alexi's father was still a handsome man for sixty-five. He had the same tall, powerful physique as his son, same thick, dark hair, only Philip's was sprinkled with grey. Helen, Alexi's mother, was probably ten years younger than her husband. She looked stylish and sophisticated in a black-and-white dress, and yet approachable, as if she was the sort of person you could talk to if you had a problem. Katie liked them both immediately.

She liked the fact that when they saw their son there were tears and effusive welcomes in Greek. Katie stood slightly back, but found herself immediately included and greeted like a long-lost daughter.

'We are just so pleased,' Alexi's mother kept saying to Katie. 'So happy for you both. Welcome to the family, Katie.'

The words touched Katie. She had never been a part of a family like this before; they were so demonstrative and warm-hearted. And they spoke to her with such genuine affection that it blew her away.

A chair was found for her at a table that was filled with food. It looked like a feast had been laid out for over two-hundred people. A glass of champagne was pressed into her hands, and everyone was speaking to her at once.

She was introduced to Alexi's two sisters. They were very attractive brunettes, both younger than him. Alesha was fifteen, Julia was twenty-six and married with a two-month-old little girl called Georgia. Obviously both girls adored their big brother; Katie watched as they flung their arms around him and he hugged them tight before being handed his niece.

It gave Katie the strangest feeling, seeing Alexi holding that baby. He looked so at home—so gentle and tender—as he rocked the child in his arms and talked to her with warmth and love in his voice. The ruthless, powerful tycoon was gone and in his place was someone Katie had never seen before. It made her heart fill with even more love for him…more love than she knew how to handle.

He would be a good dad, she thought with certainty as she tried to blink away sudden tears—a wonderful dad.

He glanced over at her, and for a moment their eyes connected through the crowds. He smiled at her.

'So, tell me all about your wedding,' his mother was demanding. 'Where exactly did you get married? When did Alexi propose?' The questions raced on.

'It's just been a complete whirlwind,' Katie answered honestly. 'I still can't believe it myself, to be honest!'

'That sounds like Alexi!' His mother laughed. 'When my son decides that he wants something, he doesn't usually like to wait.'

'So what about your family, Katie? Will they be waiting for you in England to celebrate when you get back?' Philip asked.

'Unfortunately I only have my sister, and she is in France. My mother died when I was sixteen, and I never knew my dad.'

'Well, you have us now, Katie,' Alexi's mother said, and patted her hand.

'Yes, heaven help you,' Alexi said teasingly. 'The entire family's mad.'

'Pay no attention to him,' Helen said with a smile. 'If he doesn't behave himself I shall tell some stories about the scrapes he got into when he was a little boy—things you need to know,' she laughed, and winked at Katie.

As the sun disappeared the garden was lit with twinkling lanterns, and people started to dance by the side of the swimming pool. More and more people arrived. Katie was separated from Alexi for a while as people flocked to meet her.

Alexi's father tried to pile her plate with more food. 'Really, I couldn't eat another mouthful,' she laughed. 'I'll be the size of a house.'

'Nonsense,' he'd said gruffly. 'We need to feed you up.'

Katie had to smile at that; it was such a fatherly thing to say. It was strange how at home she felt here—how accepted. She'd never felt like this before. She liked it. She liked the way Alexi's father put his arm around his wife and gave her a kiss as he walked past.

They looked happy together—as if they were still in love even after all the years of marriage.

Would Alexi ever look at her like that? she wondered suddenly. The thought made her feel quite emotional again. Must be her hormones, she thought angrily. She was never usually so weepy one moment and so happy the next...it was strange.

'Ah, so you must be the radiant bride.' A woman came to stand beside her. She was about the same age as Katie with long blonde hair and a stunning figure that she seemed proud to flaunt in a low-cut black strapless dress. 'I'm a distant cousin of Alexi's, Natasha Scollini.'

'Pleased to meet you.' Katie smiled politely.

'I have to say, I was surprised when I saw you. You're not what I was expecting.'

The comment surprised Katie. And she didn't like the woman's tone. 'So what were you expecting?' she asked curtly.

'Forgive me, Katie. I shouldn't really say it, but I was expecting you to look like Andrea. It's just Alexi was so...absolutely head over heels in love with her. Dying about her, in fact, that, well, I expected him to have fallen for someone similar.'

'I think if he had been going to do that he would have done it eight years ago, don't you?' Katie replied archly.

'Yes, you're quite right.' Natasha smiled. 'I shouldn't have said anything; I hope you'll forgive me.'

'There's nothing to forgive.' Katie shrugged.

'I saw Andrea in Athens quite recently, actually, she was between assignments, on her way to Paris,' Natasha continued. 'She looked stunning. She must be about twenty-nine now—which I suppose is old for a model—but, whatever beauty regime she is using, it certainly is working. Of course, confidence is a great beauty boost, isn't it? And being on the cover of this month's *Vogue* must be a hell of a thrill.'

Alexi's sister Julia walked over towards them and Natasha started to talk to someone else next to her before moving away.

'What was she saying?' Julia asked with barely concealed dislike.

'She was just telling me how successful and beautiful Andrea is,' Katie said wryly.

'Oh, was she indeed?' Julia shook her head. 'She'
probably as jealous as hell about you marrying Alexi. She
thought when he and Andrea divorced that she stood a
chance with him, but he was never interested in her!'

'Oh, I see.' Katie smiled, and then couldn't help asking
'So is it true that Andrea is a top model?'

'Yes. She was just starting to make a name for hersel
as a model when Alexi met her, and she's working fo
some top fashion-houses now.'

'Alexi never talks about her,' Katie murmured.

'Well, he was pretty cut up after the divorce. But it's al
in the past. It's good to see him so happy again.' She
glanced over at Katie. 'I really am so pleased for you both
And don't give anything Natasha says a second thought.'

'Give what a second thought?' Alexi asked as he
joined them.

'Natasha,' Julia informed him bluntly. 'She really i
painful!'

'Why? What has she been saying?' Alexi looked a
Katie and smiled a warm, teasing kind of smile that made
her heart dip in a very peculiar way.

'Nothing important.' Katie didn't want to start repeat
ing that conversation to him. 'This is a lovely party; it's s
kind of your parents to go to so much trouble for us.' She
changed the subject abruptly.

'Do you want to dance?' Alexi asked her suddenly.

She followed his gaze to where couples were wrapped
in each other's arms. The music was slow, the mood very
sentimental.

The thought of being held that close to him made her
ache inside.

Firmly she shook her head. 'No thank you.'

But Alexi was already reaching for her hand and leading her away. 'Excuse us, Julia,' he said over his shoulder.

As soon as they made their way onto the floor everyone gathered around them to applaud. And suddenly Katie felt like the biggest hypocrite in the world. All these people thought Alexi was in love with her—and he wasn't. He probably never would be.

The night air was warm, yet she shivered as he pulled her into his arms.

She tried to hold herself slightly apart from him.

'Relax, Katie.' He murmured the words against her ear and kissed the side of her face. Then he wrapped his arms around her, pulling her close in against him.

The gesture was probably for the audience's sake, but it felt so good that it made little pangs of desire dart deep inside her. For a moment she allowed herself to lean in against him dreamily. Allowed herself to imagine that they were an ordinary couple who had just got married because they were very much in love. Allowed herself to dream that Alexi was crazy about her.

Alexi stroked a hand down over her back. 'The evening has been a great success,' he murmured against her ear. 'Everyone loves you.'

Except the one person whose love really mattered to her.

The painful reality swirled in like the tide.

Desperately she tried to ignore it. But being in his arms like this was too pleasurable, and the bittersweet feelings wouldn't go away.

She couldn't deal with this situation, she thought suddenly, and as the music changed to another romantic ballad she pulled away from him abruptly.

'Alexi, do you think we could go now?'

He looked down into the bright blue of her eyes, and was shocked when he saw the haunted shadows of unhappiness there.

'Are you OK?' The gentleness of his voice made her feel even more wretched, but she forced herself to smile.

'Yes, just a bit tired. I think my body clock is all over the place.'

Alexi nodded and let her go. 'It's getting late anyway.' He smiled. 'And we are on our honeymoon; people can't expect us to socialise too much…'

She tried to smile back. But she just couldn't now.

It took longer than Katie had hoped to get away. They got entangled up with goodbyes. And Alexi's mother insisted that they should take food home with them.

'I have the impression she thought you were in need of a good square meal,' Alexi said with a laugh when they finally got into the car. 'The fact that I've not only got a fully stocked kitchen back at the house, but also a chef willing to cook anything we'd like, seems to be lost on her.'

'It's because she's your mother and she wants to take care of you—and you should never take that for granted,' Katie told him softly. 'Because not everyone has a relationship like that with their parents.'

Silence fell between them as the warmth and light of the house was left behind. The road was pitch-black ahead except for the silvery gleam of the powerful headlights as they cut through the countryside.

'I heard you saying tonight that you never knew your father,' Alexi said suddenly. 'That must have been tough.'

'Yes, it was.' For a moment Katie thought about the past, about how very different their upbringings were.

'What happened to him?' Alexi asked.

'Precisely nothing happened to him,' Katie informed him flatly. 'I was born, but he wasn't remotely interested. Not everyone has your sense of duty, Alexi.'

'I don't want my child out of a sense of duty, Katie,' he told her in a low tone. 'My feelings for our baby go much deeper than that.'

'Yes, of course.' She bit down on her lip.

'So did your dad walk out when you were born? Or were your parents never together?'

'They were never together.' Katie looked up at the sky. It was so bright—she had never seen the stars so clear. Something about the darkness made her relax a little. 'Lucy is really my half-sister. My mother was divorced when Lucy was three, and I don't think she ever really recovered from that divorce. Lucy's father was the real love of my mother's life, as she'd tell us on regular occasions.'

'And your father?' Alexi asked gently.

'Just an affair she had to try and make herself feel better after the divorce. And when she told him she was pregnant he didn't want to know.'

Silence stretched between them, filled with the steady thud of her heartbeats.

'The irony is that my mother always thought that Lucy's father might have come back to her, except apparently he didn't want me. I wasn't part of the equation.'

'He mustn't have really loved her, because if he had the fact that she had a child to someone else wouldn't have mattered to him,' Alexi told her gently. 'He'd have loved you, too, because you were a part of her.'

She shrugged. 'Unfortunately my mother wasn't that rational when it came to matters of the heart. She just never got over Brian. And she kept on choosing the wrong men.

They would move in and they would move out. After a few years Lucy used to get away from it occasionally by going to stay with her dad and his new wife. They were the worst times of all. Life without Lucy was…unbearable. We used to share a room, and somehow it seemed safer when she was there.'

Alexi felt his stomach churn. God alone knew what she had been through!

'Anyway, I don't know why I am telling you this.' She suddenly felt embarrassed that she had opened up to him like that. 'And my mother was a good woman; she tried very hard to do her best for me and for Lucy. It's certainly not easy being a single parent.'

Suddenly Alexi understood her fierce need for independence—she must never really have felt loved as a child. Her mother trying to apportion blame on her for her ex-husband's unwillingness to try and resolve their differences was almost barbarically cruel, to his mind. How could you blame an innocent child for being born?

He understood now how vulnerable she must have felt when she had discovered she was pregnant. He understood why she had agreed to this marriage—she would want her child to have all the love and security that she'd never had. It would be desperately important to her—more important even than her own happiness.

For a moment he remembered the way she had looked up at him when he had placed the wedding band on her finger. The shimmering vulnerability cut through him like a knife.

Obviously this marriage was the last thing she wanted, but she was desperately trying to do the right thing. She probably felt trapped and desperately unhappy, and he had compounded those feelings by demanding her hand in marriage and rushing her into it.

Alexi pulled the car into the gateway to his house, and a few moments later drew to a halt outside the front door.

He strove for something to say, something that would reassure her.

'Katie, I realise this wedding is hardly the fairy-tale romance that you probably would have wanted,' he said quietly. 'But I promise I will look after you—I will always be there for you.'

'I've told you, Alexi. I don't need looking after.' She swallowed hard and tried to make her voice sound light. 'But our baby will. And I want him or her to have everything that I didn't—and I'm not talking financially, now.'

'I realise that.'

For a second they sat in silence. Katie ached for him to reach out to her, to just take her hand even—but he didn't. And she told herself that it was for the best. Her emotions were too raw right now, and she might have said something really stupid—might have poured out her feelings for him and ruined everything!

She had to keep strong. As Alexi had said, this wasn't a fairy-tale romance, it was a business arrangement.

Nothing more.

CHAPTER TWELVE

'WOULD you print out two copies of that document and send one up to Alexi's office so he can look at it later please?' Katie asked her secretary as she tidied away some files that were cluttering up her desk.

'Is he in today?' Petra asked.

'Yes, his plane gets in at about two-thirty and he's going to come straight here.' As she said the words Katie felt a little thrill of anticipation. She hadn't seen Alexi for nearly four days; he'd been in New York on business, and she had missed him so much.

She glanced at her watch. It was twelve-thirty. She'd always sworn that she would never get hooked on a man to the point where she counted the hours and the minutes when they were apart, but that was exactly what she was doing.

Part of her was even tempted to head down to the airport to meet him. Now that really would be crazy! She was supposed to be playing it cool, she reminded herself—keeping an emotional distance. Throwing her arms around him at the airport was not recommended. He'd be running in the opposite direction in no time.

She pushed her chair back from the desk as Petra left the room, and then went to stand by the window.

The last few weeks since their wedding had passed in a bit of a blur. It had been decided that she would work from the Athens office and reside at Alexi's house in the countryside. And she liked the arrangement. It was better than being in Alexi's flat in London. She had lived there for a week when they had returned from honeymoon, and she hadn't enjoyed it. That flat belonged to Alexi's bachelor lifestyle. It was in every sense a single guy's domain. The modern, austere furnishings—the black satin sheets—all belonged to a time that Katie didn't want to even think about never mind be faced with on a daily basis.

Sometimes when she'd come in from work in the evenings there had been messages on the answer machine from old girlfriends, asking him if he was free for dinner or the theatre.

At first she had erased them in a fit of pique, but then later she had left them for when Alexi got home—usually a couple of hours later than her—just to see what he would say about them.

She needn't have worried. He'd deleted them without even listening to the complete message, and that had made her feel better—but it was disconcerting to know that women were still chasing after him even though it had been well-publicised that he was now married.

Working from the Athens office had been her idea. She needed to travel to London every few weeks, but the majority of her work could be done from here. And Alexi seemed happy to be based back in Greece. He'd already made it clear that when the baby was born he wanted Greece to be their home anyway. So he was pleased to start the arrangement immediately.

She loved being at the house on the coast. Despite its associations with his past marriage, she found she liked its tranquillity, liked the fact that Alexi wanted her to put her own stamp on it. It was the family home she'd never had and she was enjoying buying things for it, planning a nursery. And when Alexi was away sometimes she saw his sisters or his parents and she felt that she was somewhere safe—somewhere she was loved. Even if that love didn't come from her husband.

She frowned now as that thought returned like a black cloud on her sunny horizon. She wasn't going to dwell on that, she told herself fiercely.

Instead she glanced again at her watch and wondered what Alexi would say when she told him that she had bought herself a car.

He'd left a limousine at her disposal, but she'd found it strange, having someone waiting for her all the time. It wasn't her—she liked doing her own thing, driving herself. So yesterday she'd gone out and bought herself a second-hand car. And this morning she had driven herself along the scenic coast road to work and she'd enjoyed the experience.

The phone rang on her desk and she walked over to snatch it up. 'Hi, it's me.' Alexi's velvet tones sent an immediate shiver of excitement down her spine.

'Where are you ringing from? I thought you'd still be in the air.'

'There's been a technical hitch. I'm in Paris.'

'Paris?' She frowned.

'Afraid so. There's a problem at the office here, so I've had to stop off and sort it out.'

'I see.' Katie tried to swallow down her disappointment. 'So when do you think you'll get back?'

'I'm not sure. It might be tomorrow now.'

'I suppose it can't be helped.' Katie tried to sound upbeat.

and wondered if she had overdone it, because her voice sounded far too bright—he was going to guess that she was upset if she wasn't careful. 'Hey, guess what?' She changed the subject abruptly.

'What?'

'I've bought a car.'

'You have?' He sounded surprised. 'If you wanted a car you should have said. I'd have come with you and bought you one.'

'Thanks, Alexi, but I can buy my own. And it was a spur of the moment thing, anyway—I was passing a garage forecourt in that little village—you know the one down the road from your parents' house?—and I saw it, and thought it was just what I needed.'

'Well, I hope it's OK. The roads are dodgy around there. I really would have preferred it if you'd waited a while until you knew them better—'

'Alexi, it's fine. Really.' She cut across him briskly.

'I'll check it out when I get home.' He sounded resigned. 'How's Junior?'

It was the question he asked every day when he rang. It was all he was really bothered about, and it was probably the real reason behind his concern for her on the roads—but that was fine. Because at least he cared about their child, and when he or she was born there would be an even stronger bond between them.

'Everything is fine,' she told him. 'I'm booked to have a scan next week.'

'Good. I'll come with you to that.' Alexi sounded distracted now. Someone else was talking to him. Katie thought it sounded like a female voice. 'I've got to go, Katie. I'll see you soon. Take care of yourself and that baby.'

Then he was gone.

She put the phone down. He was working and it couldn't be helped, she told herself calmly as she tried to dismiss disappointment and unease. And the woman was probably a secretary, or a driver, or his accountant. She could be any number of employees.

Katie turned her attention back to work. She had never been a jealous, suspicious person and she wasn't going to turn into one either!

Somehow Katie put all thoughts of Alexi out of her mind for the rest of the afternoon, and she managed to get a lot of work done. It wasn't until she was home in the solitude of the house that the whispers of doubt started again.

Paris was a strange place to be detained. It really wasn't one of their busiest offices—it ran on a skeleton staff and there were hardly ever any problems there. Why had he been detained in Paris?

She had a shower and took herself off to bed with a cup of tea to try and relax herself—but still the thoughts went round and round in her head until she had to get up again.

Andrea was in Paris.

The thought came into her head from nowhere. The woman at the party had told her that Andrea was off on a modelling assignment in Paris.

It was a coincidence, she told herself. Alexi and Andrea had been divorced for a long time. If they'd wanted to get back together they would have done it by now.

But maybe they didn't want to get back together; maybe they just wanted to meet up every now and then for sex. That was the kind of arrangement Alexi liked.

Katie felt sick suddenly. She went into the kitchen and got herself a glass of water and then padded out to the terrace.

The night was so hot it was sticky. She sat on the swing chair and looked out at the sea. The roll of the surf was soothing.

She was being fanciful. Alexi was on business and he would be home soon.

Flashes of lightning lit up the sky suddenly as if someone was switching a light bulb on and off, and there was a low growl of thunder. Katie watched the dramatic play of light across the sky, watched the way it lit up the sea in a surreal moment of silver. It scared her and fascinated her at the same time. Then there was an almighty roar that was almost deafening, it was so loud.

She got up to go back inside, and that was when the first twinges of pain hit her stomach. As she went upstairs it was just a niggling discomfort, but by the time she had reached the bedroom it was steadily getting worse.

She sat down on the edge of the bed and took deep breaths. What was the matter with her? *Was she losing the baby?*

The thought tore through her almost as violently as the storm raging outside.

Desperately she tried to calm herself, but tears sprung to her eyes as another pain tore through her and she doubled up into a protective ball. She couldn't lose her baby—she just couldn't. It would be the end of everything!

For a few minutes she didn't think she could bear it. She listened to the sound of the thunder resounding through the mountains like cannonfire and breathed deeply. Breathing seemed to help. The pain started to recede. Her mobile was sitting next to the bed, and she reached for it to try and ring Alexi. She needed to hear his voice—she needed him.

A voice message said his number was unavailable.

She tried to ring his parents' house but there was no

reply, just an answer machine. She started to leave a message saying she wasn't feeling well—then changed her mind and hung up. What could they do? They weren't even home! And she knew his sister Julia and her husband were away on holiday for a couple of days.

She tried to think rationally. The pain was easing even more now and there was no blood.

Was she well enough to drive? Perhaps she could get herself to the hospital. She knew where it was; she'd been for routine blood tests a couple of days ago.

Katie tried to stand up. Surprisingly she felt all right. Maybe the pain had been nothing to worry about. She put her hand protectively on her stomach. But to be on the safe side it might be best to get to a doctor. Quickly she reached for a pair of linen trousers that she had left on the chair and replaced her nightdress with a T-shirt, gathered her bag, phone and car keys and headed for the door.

For a while she felt OK. She got into her car and started the engine. Everything was going to be fine, she told herself over and over as she headed out along the winding coast road.

Fork lightning was gashing across the sky in front of her, illuminating the darkness. She drove a few miles, following the twisty road slowly and carefully. And then the rain started.

One moment she could see clearly, the next it was like someone had placed her inside a carwash where the outside world ceased to exist, and she was enveloped in a watery world all of her own. She put the windscreen wipers on at full speed but still they wouldn't clear it. All she could do was pull the car over to the side of the road and stop.

It was probably a cloudburst that would last for a minute and then pass, she reassured herself, trying to fight down the feelings of unease. But the minutes ticked away, and there was no respite.

The storm sounded as if it was directly overhead now. The thunder was so violent she imagined it shook her car.

Katie was aware that her situation was not a safe one. Although there was very little traffic on this road, if something was still moving along the highway it might not see her and hit her. She tried to reassure herself that other drivers would be in the same predicament, and would have pulled over to stop, but even so she didn't like it.

She put on the light inside the car—every little thing helped, she thought. Then she just waited and waited for the storm to pass.

The rain was easing a little when the pain started again. It just gnawed at first—but it was there.

Katie put her hand on her stomach. She was into the second trimester of her pregnancy now and they said that the risk of miscarriage was lower once you passed that point. She and Alexi had planned to tell his parents this weekend.

She felt her eyes blur with tears as the pain started to increase again. She wanted her child so much, wanted to hold her and love her. Wanted to be a mother.

If she lost her baby it would be the end of her dreams and hopes for the future—her family life—her marriage!

She reached for her mobile phone and dialled Alexi's number again. She didn't know what he could do—he was probably still in Paris—but just hearing his voice and talking to him would be something. But his phone didn't even ring now. She glanced at the dial and noticed with horror that she didn't have a signal. She was obviously at a point in the road where the mountains blocked out the transmitters.

She hung up and started to cry in earnest—she couldn't

help it. She was tired of being strong, of trying to pretend that everything was going to be all right. Maybe it wasn't.

The house was ablaze with lights when Alexi got home. He stood in the hallway and called up the stairs. 'Katie, honey, where are you?'

There was no answer. 'Katie?' He looked through the doorway into the kitchen. It was deserted.

Thinking that she might be in bed asleep, he put the kettle on and looked out of the window. The storm had been fierce; it had delayed him landing in Athens, and he'd been forced to wait a while before being able to drive back along the coast. The road had been completely impassable in parts due to flooding, forcing him to make a long detour.

At least the storm had been late at night and not earlier, otherwise he'd have worried about Katie driving back in it. He hoped the car she'd bought was OK. Come to think about it, where was the car? He hadn't seen a vehicle when he'd driven up.

Alexi glanced further along the driveway but he couldn't see another car. He headed out of the kitchen and up the stairs. The lights in the bedroom were on, and it looked as if Katie had been in bed, because the bedclothes were thrown back and there was a full cup of tea on the bedside table. He put his hand against the side of it but it was cold.

'Katie?' He wandered through to the *en suite* bathroom, but no sign of her there either. 'Katie?' He went back to the doorway into the corridor and called her. Then he noticed her nightshirt on the floor.

He frowned, quickly took out his mobile phone and

dialled her. There was no reply and no sound of a phone ringing in the house.

He'd just hung up when his phone rang, and hurriedly he answered it, hoping it was Katie. But it was his mother.

'Alexi, we've just got in and there is a message on our answer machine from Katie telling us she is not feeling well. Is she OK? We've been trying to ring her but there is no reply.'

Fear wasn't an emotion Alexi was familiar with but he felt it now—twisting through him like a serpent. 'I've just got in and she's not here.'

There was silence as they both thought about the storm that had raged a short while ago and the conditions of the roads.

If she'd driven somewhere in that weather she could be at the bottom of a gully somewhere. The thought pounded through Alexi's consciousness, and he raked his hand through his hair, trying desperately to rid himself of it.

'What sort of car did she buy, do you know?' he grated suddenly.

'No, she didn't say, and I didn't see it. I think she said it was red—yes, she definitely said it was red, I remember now.'

'I'll go find her.'

'Ring me as soon as you know anything.'

Alexi headed out of the house at a sprint. The rain had stopped now, but the thunder was still growling, and lightning was still flicking through the darkness of the night.

If she hadn't been feeling well she probably would have headed back to Athens towards a hospital. With grim determination Alexi turned his car along the road in that direction.

If anything had happened to her he didn't know what he would do! He'd never forgive himself. He shouldn't have left her.

His hands gripped the steering wheel as memories flicked through him of how she'd looked when they'd said goodbye four days ago. She'd been almost radiantly beautiful, the sun shimmering over the chestnut lights in her hair, her skin glowing with health.

They'd laughed about her sudden craving for ice cream. 'At least I'm not eating it with pickled onions,' she'd said with a smile.

He remembered taking her into his arms and kissing her. He remembered the way she had looked up at him.

Something twisted and knotted in his gut.

There was an emergency-services truck ahead towing a vehicle out of a ditch. He slowed the car and scanned the small group of people standing by the roadside, but Katie wasn't amongst them.

A police officer waved him over and he stopped and wound down his window to speak to him.

'The road is pretty bad ahead, sir, I wouldn't advise going any further.'

'I'm going to have to, officer,' Alexi told him bluntly. 'My wife could be along there somewhere—she's pregnant and alone—I need to get to her.'

He didn't wait for a reply, just put up the window and continued.

There had been a landslide a little further along, and he had to transverse around it. That was when he saw the red car wedged in between the landfall on the road. The car itself looked undamaged. It still had its headlights on and a light on inside.

He left his car with the engine still running and darted across towards it, wrenching the door open.

'Katie? Katie, honey, are you OK?' She was sitting sideways in the passenger seat—her feet up on the seat, hugging her knees against her chest, her head buried down onto them, so that all he could see was the glossy fall of her hair.

She looked up and he could see that she had been crying, and his heart turned over.

'Katie. Are you OK?' he asked again. His voice sounded raw even to his own ears.

Her face crumpled. 'I think I'm losing the baby, Alexi,' she whispered.

'Come on, honey, don't cry.' He kneeled in on the driver's seat. 'Can you move?'

She shook her head and then watched as he tried to use his phone to call an ambulance. 'There's no signal,' she told him roughly. 'None! It's no good…'

She was right. He snapped the phone closed and then reached for her. Putting one hand under her knees and one around her back he gently slid her towards him and then lifted her out.

'I'm sorry,' she whispered as she curled her arms up and around his neck. 'I'm so sorry, Alexi. I didn't know what to do…and I know how much you want this baby. I do, too.'

'It'll be OK.' He smoothed her hair back from her face and kissed her cheek. He didn't know what to say to her; he had never felt more inadequate in all of his life. 'I'm here now—I'll take care of you.' His voice grated unevenly on a hard lump of emotion in his throat.

'I've been having pains like contractions for the last couple of hours,' she told him. 'I don't think it will be OK.'

She sounded exhausted. 'Try and relax—are you still in pain?' He carried her over towards his car.

'No, not now, but it keeps coming in waves.' She put her arms more tightly around his neck, breathing him in. It was so good to be held by him, to feel his strength. She wanted never to let him go.

Alexi tried to think practically—and not to dwell on the emotions raging inside him. He managed to open the passenger door and bent down to put her into the seat.

For a moment she didn't let go of him.

'Katie.' He crouched down beside her and gently untwisted her arms from round his neck.

'We'll get you to hospital and get you the best medical attention we can find, OK?' He smiled slightly.

For a moment their eyes held. 'Money doesn't fix every problem, Alexi,' she whispered. 'But we already know that…don't we?'

His eyes darkened. 'Come on, baby…' He stroked a hand down over her cheek and she closed her eyes weakly as a flood of tears sparkled afresh, blurring her vision. 'You need to keep strong,' he said softly.

'Yes, I know. I keep telling myself that.' Her eyes flicked open and met with his. 'But if I lose the baby then our marriage is over, isn't it, Alexi?' She whispered the words. 'We both know that, so there is no point in pretending anything else, is there?'

For a second she saw a muscle pulsing in the side of his jawline. 'You can't talk like that, Katie,' he said quietly. 'You just can't!'

He closed the door and walked round to the driver's side.

He was right, she shouldn't have said that! Because voicing it made it all the more real. And the thought of losing their child was too much to bear for Alexi. She'd seen it in his eyes.

She bit down on her lip and tried to concentrate on her breathing as the pain inside her started again.

CHAPTER THIRTEEN

KATIE had looked pale and fragile against the white of the hospital bed-linen, her eyes an impossible shade of blue. The image stayed in Alexi's mind as he paced outside in the corridor.

They were giving her a scan and she had refused to have him present. He'd been about to insist, but something about the pleading way she had looked at him had stopped him.

So now here he was, pacing outside the room like some draconian father-to-be.

A nurse left the room without glancing in his direction and then hurried back in a few moments later.

He didn't think he could bear this.

He raked a hand through his hair. He'd made so many mistakes, he realised suddenly—he'd been blind and stupid...

'If I lose the baby then our marriage is over, isn't it, Alexi?' Katie's words played over and over through his mind like a broken tape-recording.

What the hell was he doing, waiting out here? He needed to be with her.

The door opened and the doctor came out. 'You can go in now. She's very tired so take it easy on her, OK?'

Katie watched as he walked towards the bed. She had never seen him so drawn, and her heart twisted with pain.

She remembered when he'd found her tonight—when he'd pulled her out of that car and wrapped her within the strength of his arms. She remembered how safe she had suddenly felt—until she'd remembered that she wasn't safe at all...that without the baby she was nothing to him.

She swallowed hard. She hadn't wanted him in the room when the doctors were running their tests, because she'd felt if they told her that their baby was dead she couldn't handle it—that she needed to prepare herself before she could face him. That she needed every piece of inner strength to deal with what had happened.

'Alexi, it's—it's OK.' She whispered the words tremulously. 'There is still a heartbeat. Our baby's still fighting—she's still alive.'

For a moment there was a look of intense relief on his face, a look that melted her heart. 'I'm sorry I kept you outside—I just...' She bit down on her lip. 'I just couldn't handle your disappointment, Alexi...not along with everything else.'

He sat down on the side of her bed and reached for her hand.

'It's still touch and go, though,' she told him, trying to sound brave. 'They need to do more tests—they say the next twenty-four hours will be crucial.'

His hand tightened on hers.

'But at least I'm in the right place now.' She tried to sound positive. 'At least there is a chance now.'

'Yes, at least there is a chance.' For a moment his eyes raked over the beauty of her face, drinking her in. He noticed how even though she was so pale, and obviously in turmoil, her chin was tipped up and the old determination was back in her eyes.

'God, Katie, can you ever forgive me...?' he whispered suddenly.

'Forgive you?' She looked at him in puzzlement.

'For trapping you into this marriage.' He said the words so softly she could hardly hear him. 'For making you rush into something that you really didn't want—'

'Alexi, I want what is best for our baby!' Her eyes widened. 'I *need* what is best for our baby.'

She said the words with such anguish that his heart twisted savagely.

'I know.' He cut across her fiercely. 'I know you've put our child's happiness above your own.' He shook his head. 'I can see it in your eyes. I can sense it sometimes just in the quietness of a moment when I glance at you—'

'Alexi, don't—'

'And I've been such an idiot!' He cut across her firmly. 'I realised something tonight.' He stroked a hand down over the side of her cheek. 'Katie, I realised that, as deeply devastated as I would be at losing our baby, it would be nothing beside the pain of losing you...'

For a moment Katie wondered if she had misheard him.

'I love you, Katie.' He said the words huskily, his voice raw and almost broken.

She had never heard him sound like that before, and it made the tears well up even more inside her.

'Am I dreaming this?' she asked uncertainly, and he smiled.

'You're not dreaming, and I think I probably loved you from the first moment we met. Do you remember in the shipping office, surrounded by all those damn files and business plans?'

'Of course I remember,' she whispered. 'But I don't think you fell in love with me—you let me go…you let me walk away…' Her voice trembled now as she remembered the end of their affair.

'Yes, and I was stupid, Katie!' His voice was fierce for a moment, his eyes burning into hers. 'I was so tied up in the past that I couldn't see what was right in front of me!'

'You were still in love with Andrea.' She nodded. 'I realise that now.'

He looked at her in surprise. 'Nothing could be further from the truth, Katie. I wasn't still in love with Andrea. I got over that years ago!'

'I don't think so.' She shook her head.

'Katie.' He took hold of her other hand. 'I was badly burnt by Andrea. Yes, I did love her when we married. I was…besotted, I suppose is the word.'

Katie nodded and tried not to look like that hurt her…but it did. It hurt so much. 'And you are still not over her.'

'Believe me, Katie, I'm over her.' His voice was grim for a second. 'But you are right in one way. My experience with Andrea did cloud my judgement of the future. I never wanted to feel like that again.' He stared at her. 'Never wanted to put myself on the line like that again, because it was too painful.'

Katie nodded. She knew how that felt. 'What happened between you?' she whispered. 'What happened in your marriage that made you feel like that?'

For a moment she didn't think Alexi was going to answer her. 'You mean apart from the fact that she had an abortion without telling me?' He shrugged, and Katie knew he was trying to play things down, but she could see the pain in his eyes now. 'She didn't even tell me she was pregnant. Just booked herself into some clinic and told me she was away on a photo shoot.'

Suddenly Katie remembered his anger when she'd told him she was pregnant—remembered that look in his eye when he thought she'd been hiding it from him—and everything started to fall into place.

'Alexi, I'm sorry—and I got it so wrong, didn't I, when I accused you of never wanting children.'

'It's not your fault, I should have told you.' Alexi shrugged. 'It's just not something I wanted to talk about to anyone.'

'I can understand that,' she said softly. 'And the gossips made a kind of Chinese-whispers thing out of it and got it the wrong way around.'

'Better than them knowing the truth,' Alexi murmured. 'I tried to understand her reasons, Katie—I really did,' he grated unevenly. 'And I forgave her. It is a woman's prerogative—it was her decision ultimately—but the fact that she couldn't even talk about it to me…' He shook his head. 'Apparently she had been offered a modelling contract that would launch her into the big time. And it was all she ever wanted.'

There was silence between them for a moment. 'Anyway, we put it behind us and carried on,' Alexi said with a sigh. 'I still wanted so much to make the marriage work, and I understood her need for a career. But there came a point where I realised I just couldn't go on.' His eyes met with hers. 'Because it seemed Andrea would do anything to get that career—and that included sleeping with anyone to further it.'

Katie saw the flare of fierce anger in his eyes, but also the pain, and she understood suddenly his reluctance to love again—to put his heart on the line. Understood his pride and the walls he had built around himself.

'Alexi, I'm so sorry—I didn't realize.'

'How could you, when I couldn't even mention her name without reinforcing the need inside me to keep emotions under tight control?' He shook his head and then his eyes softened as he looked at her. 'And all the time I had someone like you in my life—someone gentle and loving, someone who'd been through so much herself and would even put her life on hold just for her child's happiness.'

'Alexi, I—'

'No, let me say this, Katie—I realise you didn't want to marry me, but please—please let me try to make this work. Let me try to make things right, and even—God forbid that we lose this child—please don't let it break us apart. Because I couldn't bear that—I really couldn't.'

'Alexi, I have to tell you something.' She wiped the tears away from her face and looked at him through shimmering eyes. 'I'm not as altruistic as you seem to think.'

'You're not?' He looked at her doubtfully as if he didn't believe a word of that, and she smiled.

'No.' She shook her head. 'I married you because I was expecting our child. But most of all, I married you because I loved you. I've always loved you.'

For a moment he looked at her as if he could hardly believe what she was saying to him.

'You're not feeling trapped?'

'Oh, Alexi, I just wanted you to feel the same way. It was tearing me apart, loving you so much and thinking that those feelings would never be returned.'

Suddenly she found herself wrapped in his arms, held tightly. 'Katie, forgive me…I love you so much.'

He turned his head and kissed her, and for a moment Katie just clung to him, kissing him with every ounce of love and passion in her soul.

'Tell me again,' she whispered as he pulled back. 'Tell me how much you love me.'

'Let me see…' He smiled playfully. 'Only to the sun and back…and maybe once around again.'

EPILOGUE

THE snow was thick on the ground and frozen icicles shimmered from the trees in the orchard. Greece had never known such a cold winter. But soon it would be spring, with the promise of the long, hot days ahead.

There was so much to look forward to, Katie thought as she turned away from the window with a smile; so much she had to be thankful for. For a moment her eyes moved around the room, taking in the log fire and the people who were talking and laughing. Her family.

Sometimes she couldn't believe how lucky she was. Especially when she looked over and caught Alexi's eye and he smiled at her, that special smile that he reserved only for her.

Then her eyes drifted down to the child that he held in his arms, and her heart felt like it would just burst with happiness.

She walked across towards them now. 'I don't know what this surprise is that you have planned for me,' she said, reaching to kiss him. 'But, really, you will have to stop buying me presents and spoiling me. I couldn't be any happier, Alexi—I don't need anything else.'

Alexi smiled back at her. 'But I know there is one thing

that will make this day perfect—so keep looking out of the window and you will see that I'm right.'

Katie's eyes moved down to their son. Theon Philip Alexander Demetri was due to be christened at three-thirty this afternoon. She didn't think the day could be any more perfect.

She still couldn't believe that life could feel this good—that she had been so lucky. It had been a very difficult pregnancy, and she'd had to have a lot of bed rest. But Alexi had helped her through it, and with his love and support she'd gone on to deliver their fine, healthy little boy. Katie's eyes shimmered with love as her eyes drifted down over the little cherub, so perfect in a white christening robe that had been handed down through the Demetri family for two generations.

'In fact, life is so perfect it almost scares me,' she whispered softly. 'All that's missing, of course, is my sister…'

She trailed away as she heard a car pulling up outside. Then she looked up at Alexi. 'You didn't…?' she asked breathlessly.

He nodded. 'We couldn't have the christening without Lucy, could we? She's a very important godmother.'

'Alexi, I love you so much.' She flung her arms around him, and for a moment the three of them were held close.

'And I love you, Katie.' Alexi murmured the words and crushed his lips against hers. 'More than words could ever say.'

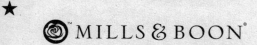